OTUS IN BETULACEÆ

OTUS IN BETULACEÆ

A Novel By

ANDERS M. SVENNING

Adelaide Books
New York / Lisbon
2018

OTUS IN BETULACEÆ
a novel
by Anders M. Svenning

Copyright © 2018 by Anders M. Svenning
Cover design © 2018 Adelaide Books

Published by Adelaide Books, New York / Lisbon
adelaidebooks.org

Editor-in-Chief
Stevan V. Nikolic

For any information, please address Adelaide Books
at info@adelaidebooks.org
or write to:
Adelaide Books
244 Fifth Ave. Suite D27
New York, NY, 10001

ISBN13: 978-0-9996451-9-2
ISBN10: 0-9996451-9-6

Printed in the United States of America

2017

It had been high noon for fifteen or twenty minutes for Pete Tsiminis, who was glancing at works, made of this and that, metalloids, precious stones, and gold leaf—and it had become high noon for the duration of his walk throughout the collection of jewelry and pottery, and the high noon did not shift from second to second, nor did it revert its sunrays into seeming angles, with the dust motes and viscosity. It stayed high noon throughout twelve o'clock P.M. in the venue in New York City, where Pete Tsiminis had been visiting, and it stayed high noon throughout the three o'clock show at the theatre, and it stayed high noon throughout the evening, in the flight back north to the Canadian province in which he lived.

He was a young person, ten or eleven years of age, and had, upon entering New York City, been granted a precocious glimpse into the disparaged divide in between traditionalist living, the routine and logistics of Man, and the virile and mechanistic contrivance, which was enveloped with the former, and which was of progeny—from the wheels, which enabled a kinetic metropolis, on the first afternoon of his stay, to the metalloid craftsmanship, inside case after case of aged and immaculate pieces from the birthplace of religion, that is Byzantion—and he had been enraptured by that exchange, in the hard wood floor anteroom, which held the innumerable pieces, and in that ambience of a naturalistic and celebratory tempest, that he was not able to escape high noon, and, in a likeness in him and in his sub-stratum of mannishness, was unable to relinquish that hour.

Pete Tsiminis had a drink. It had been in the anteroom of the museum, where he and his family had been visiting. The drink had come from the fountain, and it was cold, which was pleasant to Pete Tsiminis and his thirst. It had not reached high noon, not yet; it was eleven-fifty A.M. when Pete took that drink of water from the fountain and made cold his thoracic cavity with the cold water and carried the cold with him into the collection of Byzantine pieces, one of which attracted him in such surety he could not dissent the action of walking over to the piece and taking a look at it in closeness—a chalice, rimmed with rubies around its base, which was flat; and sapphire, too, adorned the chalice. It had been when Pete was gazing into the chalice, with its stones reflecting his countenance back at him, the clock in the corner of the museum room turned to high noon, and the clock down the street in the chapel became high noon, and the clock in the restaurant where Pete and his parents ate and the subway station clock, which Pete noticed made an ubiquitous expression towards him changed to high noon, the hands of the clock in the museum room upright and enmeshed as one hand, the church bells tolling and the chimes striking off twelve cerebral and pernicious chimes, and the clock in the restaurant where Pete and his family had eaten and the subway station clock, which Pete noticed had made an ubiquitous expression towards him, assumed the collinear posit, a certain separation in between the temporal and the taciturn, and stayed that way, maniacal and sovereign.

It had feigned from the memory of Pete Tsiminis, but four years prior, the clock in the school, which he attended, had assumed the same posit, with the two hands at apex, and insinuating a high noon for he, who was excitable at that hour, because in fifteen minutes the class would depart to the Betulaceæ forest, that is the birch wood, just east of the school, and the class, or lot, which was an appropriate term with which to don them—they were a boisterous group— would traverse the wood and find, deeper in the Betulaceæ that which was the item in question, pellets of owls, and the class, or lot did not have a preconception of the journey into the wood, nor did they find themselves in the know of the goings on, which had taken place not one hour prior that titular piquant and high noon, and the apprehensiveness did not take its leave, nor find residence in one of the students, but in all of the students in simultaneity, a distal contiguity.

One hour prior the students taking their seats on the school bus, faculty had gone out and into the birch wood and had placed pellets of owls in seeming yet conspicuous locations, where the students would discover and collect their pellets for the subsequent operation—the finite fingers of many a student tearing in twain many a pellet, exposing the endoskeleton of just as well any species of Animalia, having been consumed and regurgitated by the Otus, from Rodentia to, in particular cases, Batrachians, the skeletons of which the students would reconstrue into two-dimensional skeletons, in their available axes and in their weird and medieval pertinence.

The grasses of the wood transmuted themselves into soils and gnarled grounds, the students traversing with abandon the Betulaceæ in sublime desire of the pellets of the Otus, in conviviality. The pellets of the Otus materialized themselves for the students as if of their own accord, an exchange, which had arrived, and which was conducive to extolment.

In the hour following the arrival of the garrulous lot, many a hand found themselves in the apprehension of the pellets of Otus, all the hands of which did not include Pete Tsiminis's hand, which had become tentative, and which had begun to perspire in its ineffectuality—the pellets of Otus were evasive and they, in all of Pete Tsiminis's contrivance, seemed to have dematerialized as sure as he had done the contrary in this wood, this Betulaceæ; and what were to happen should he not arrive with a pellet at the rendezvous?

He was quite lonesome in that expanse, empty of hand and not in the possession of that which was the item which attracted him here, the item relevant to not only the approaching three hours of education, but also in the approaching three decades of the corporeal existence, which was to house Pete Tsiminis through pneumonia in his late twenties; and through three children, two of which of one girl and the third of another girl; and through a compound fracture over an afternoon of skiing through the streets of Red Bay, behind his acquaintance's Chrysler, on skis, literally skis, with wheels screwed into the bottoms of the skis; and literally through the whale family in the harbor, at full sail—an intricate collection of causations, which recapitulated little, and which incited circulation in the fluidic avenues of Babylon, the carved and seeming pit of an apricot, valleys of electrical nonsense, aberrations in already outstanding anomalies, in between the hand and the stone it made nonpareil, and schemas of impressions and wax and chartreuse, all of which were touching and all of which were close together and all of which were in proximity, as vestigial balustrades.

1923

It had been Panagiotis's most appreciable day of the week, Deftera, that is Monday, and it was a day of consequential Providence, the morning having teetered over the top of that parabola, and thickening in substantiality in the way Byzantion had been known to thicken in its amplified descenesion, the proino having been consumed, that is the breakfast having been consumed by he, Panagiotis, and his compatriot, who, too, enjoyed with her breakfast of bread and cucumbers, wine, and who was named Santeia, a girl, who had become, in that peculiar and mid-afternoon stagnation, animated and so much so one could call her hysterical, in that she, on that morning, had declared Deftera, that is Monday, the most pugnacious day of the week, because of its density and because of its immobility— which was the same in regards to the procession traveling north and west—a statement, which Panagiotis had, with fervency, retorted, in conviviality.

"Monday is the most appreciable day in the week, Santeia. You are a woman. You should comprehend Monday is the most appreciable day in the week. It is not a disconcerting perspective to possess, in this day and in the circumstance in which we find ourselves."

"Pano, the morning is fat and disagreeable," Santeia had said on that morning. "The afternoon is going to be even more aggravating."

"If this Monday morning is fat and disagreeable, then this procession is Monday, because we are as so," said Panagiotis, who was referring to the people—the wagons, the Animalia, the salvagablity of their former home, and the citizens of Constantinople—the city, in all of actuality, traversing the mountainous terrain, in a decision to void the manifestation, which had been subject to intrusion from the east, and which was the birthplace of religion, known as Constantinople and Byzantion.

It was Panagiotis and Santeia, who were residing in the small vessel, which was to transport them to the western Byzantion, and which was locomotive by means of two donkeys, not at all cognizant of what was preceding them, not in terms of their masters, and not in terms of the two million individuals, who were abandoning Constantinople, and not in terms of Constantinople and six centuries of progeny and six centuries of semblance preceding those six centuries, and not in terms of the total severity.

"We are not Monday. We are not Tuesday. We are not Wednesday. We are Samigina."

"There is an island in the west."

"There are many islands in the west."

"Not so close west, but father west, much farther west."

"In America west?"

"Not so far west."

"What is the island called?"

"The island is called Bermuda. The people call it otherwise, per happenstance."

"How did you find this island."

"The map."

"Do they have schools in Bermuda, Pano? Do they have churches, Pano? Do they have theatres, Pano? Do they have pastitsio, Pano?"

"You could make pastistio in Bermuda and the people of the island would enjoy it, per happenstance."

"Pastisio is not my dish."

"Not yet. Not yet."

"I don't like pastistio in the least."

"You have to make it well and then baby it with your words and regard it, knowing it is a worthy dish, make noises at it and faces, too. Pastisio is what gave Byzantion its prescience. Pastistio is the receptor of all baby. Baby pastistio with your words and the pastitiso will turn out well."

"Byzantion has not prescience and not for many, many years."

"That is why there is pastisio."

"I'd rather baby kotopoulo."

"It is the same with kotopoulo. Baby it and then make noises at it and make faces at it and it will turn out well, knowing it is a worthy dish."

"I would rather eat the wing of the Seraphim."

"It has the gout, knowing it is a swarthy bitch."

"My breath has smelled of shit the past four weeks and nobody's there."

"It is the approximately equal sign, knowing it is a short haul brothel."

"Stefangianopoulou is considering traversing ahead of us all and doing a few chores in the villages ahead of us all."

"Stefangianopoulou can do what he needs. He has never done otherwise. Nobody can coerce him different— the only person who comes to mind who may coerce him different than what he needs to do is that girl back home, in the city, the girl he collected from the husbandry. She has been lost in this miasma. She is better off forgetting about Stefangianopoulou because he has well forgotten about her, the bimbo."

"He had forgotten about her even before he left the city."

"Yes, you are correct about that."

"Yes, I am correct about that and many other things, one of which is this monkey lung."

"Stefangianopoulou and I were collecting our belongings in the streets, picking up what we could before departing, and this Ottoman, speaking of monkeys, came up to us and asked us to give him our belongings and this—"

"Nobody has told me this."—and Stefangianopoulou kicked him in the mouth and walked away, walking backwards, saying, 'Saggitary, asshole. Saggitary, asshole.' He cares not what happens in between he and Samigina."

The lot traversed onwards, in its constancy, within which were shining exchanges in between the young and the wizened, the rotten and the fresh, the gallant and the retarded, the note and the chromatic; and he who was in question, Stefangianopoulou had ridden up, riding the Equus caballus, which would arrive him in three locations, in subsequence.

"Kali mera."

"Kali mera, Stefangianopoulou."

"Kali mera, Pano."

"Kali mera, Stefangianopoulou."

"We are headed north and reaching a few villages, Harito and I, on this morning to do a few chores before this calamity hits the area."

"What are your objectives?" asked Santeia.

"They are a few."

"Thank you for your precision."

"Parakalo."

Panagiotis said, "The villages here on forth are manacles for mounted peoples. They will kill anybody they think is an Ottoman."

"What is a manacle?" said Santeia.

Panagiotis said, "It is that into which one steps, shattering your feet."

Stefangianopoulou said, "There is no worry. All will be well and we know the people of the villages and they know us. It is not a wanton pursuit. It is best to arrive in candor."

Stefangianopoulou was riding slow beside the wagon, which had inside of it Panagiotis and Santeia, and Panagiotis could well see the specimen was walking quite too slow for comfortability; even the Animalia were recognizing the dejected nature of the scenario, and nobody was able to seduce them otherwise, not with vegetables and not with sugar, which was becoming rarer and more a novelty on the travels the matter—the bread and cucumbers and wine, which had been consumed by Panagiotis and Santeia at proino were, too, disparaged commodities, in that former citizens of Constantinople, who were once quite sufficient in their necessities, and who were quite in the apprehension of contentedness, were beginning to venture into the barabaric notion of the consumption of the flesh of Man and in deprecability—the Animalia and the citizenry and the geologics all in angst and all in counteraction, a surety, which was not apart from dismissivity, and which was not too far delineated from traitorous and territorial travesty. The bomb, which had imploded, and then which had exploded, was not a bomb of pressurized inertia—if it were, the procession would not have been in motion, propelled by vagary—and the bomb was quite evasive and peripheral. The bomb had been planted in the city, not within the walls of the architecture and not in the gardens, but more so in the myocardia and the gluten and the epithelial tissues of the citizens, a bomb, which would lie, in the visceral holes of Babylon and in consequentiality. The problem, which autosuggested itself, in the minds of men was, In what hour was that decision made, the decision to relinquish home and the decision to relinquish agapi?—in what pit thy seest thee, Beëlzebub? From what height thy have fallen?—and the answers were the questions, which autosuggested themselves in the minds of the others, Where is the meat? Where is the bread I have lain on the floor? In which hour shall he expire, he who has expired before and has expired twice and thrice and he who has not common fate, and where will he expend his fatalistic fulmination?—all inabilities and all opportunities to establish communicæ evaporated in the heathen sun. The small peoples of the granular stain produced optimistic exchanges, in regards to raillery and in regards to nonsense and in lips of tinsel and in regards to jubilance, making all contradictory and making all blatant ignorance.

In this point in the journey north and west, all of importance was the number of onions remaining and the location of the next cup of fermented juice, which was quite at hand, in the time Panagiotis said, "1924 is imminent. We will apprehend our own in 1924. There is no alternative to the fact I do state in 1923, Santeia. There is a threshold and it is relevant."

Santeia looked at him quite hard, and she said, "It is 1923, Pano. You are correct about that. It is good to hear you speaking in accurateness. 1923 is relevant and I would suggest you maintain 1923 for all it has left."

"We should have apprehended our own in 1923."

"Nobody apprehends their own in 1923."

"Then why not 1922?"

Stefangianopoulou was riding beside the small wagon. Stefangianopoulou said, "1922 was a good year."

"What makes a year good, Stefangianopoulou?"

Panagiotis said, "Good years are made of good decisions. Good decisions are those decisions, which take you with them. They have a knowledge of their own. They take you to good places."

"Then, this is a good place, Pano?" said Santeia, who was referring to the noisy swatch, of which they were a part. "Is that what you are insinuating?"

"We are all taking one another to the same place. We are all decisive in our intentions, are we not? We are all good, are we not? This skatoulismata is good."

"At kilometer two hundred is was tolerable," Santeia said. "At kilometer two hundred and one it was bad. At kilometer two hundred and fifty it was worse, and at kilometer one thousand kuruş it is going to a floundering idiot."

"At kilometer one thousand and one it will be good," said Panagiotis.

Stefangianopoulou said, from his pervasive specimen, "Popularity is the black people; the black people is the *Frankfurter Würstchen*; popularity is the *Frankfurter Würstchen*. Your words make no sense at all. What is good about this movement? What would be good is the bread you have in that box in my saddle bag, which is the reason I came here."

"Don't blame me for my optimism, Stefangianopoulou. Blame somebody blame the Arch Duke Franz Ferdinand. Don't blame me for my pansophism. Bring home some bread in your return."

"Nein."

Panagiotis opened the box, of which Stefangianopoulou had spoken, and he took the three-quarters of bread loaf remaining, which was snug on the side of the box, among belongings—silver cups and literature written by Constantinople literaries, leather gloves and a rolling pin and writing utensils, shoes and blouses and empty sacks, and stained glass, which Panagiotis had made in his childhood, and unrefined cotton and silverware and chamomile were in the box, of which Stefangianopoulou had spoken—and Panagiotis threw the three-quarters of bread loaf remaining into the chest of Stefangianopoulou, and Harito, then, had ridden up on his specimen Equus caballus and joined, just for a second. Stefangianopoulou and Harito were off and far ahead of the wagon, which retained Panagiotis and Santeia, within thirty seconds and in colloquy.

Panagiotis had been asked by his mother to join the army. The exchange was before their removal from Constantinople. In all of reality, Panagiotis's mother did not ask him to join the army, but more so suggested it as a means of validity in everything they had created for themselves and as a means to make of principle the Ottoman nonsensicality.

Panagiotis did disagree. His mother was quite predisposed to antics—one may well call her a zealot—and Panagiotis, while rather stark in his reply, withstood the notion that his mother was antiquated and had the best intentions for the populace, though, perhaps, not her own Panagiotis, who would meet a death in surety in the inevitability which was battle, and who responded to the suggestion, in the outside table, "I do not ingest that which makes fools fools, Mama. I am not a degenerate, nor am I a soldier. Soldiers are soldiers for their own reason and of their own accord, as far as I'm concerned, and I am not going to go into a battle, or an exchange with the Ottoman army for gallantry. In the streets of the city and in spontaneity I would fight, but I'm not going to fight to fight."

"You have spoken ill of the Ottomans."

"And yet, I was not ingesting that which makes fools fools."

"Were you drunk?"

"I'm a rascal." Panagiotis had been drinking when he said the proclaimed assumption—"I'm a rascal"—although he was not drunk when talking ill against the Ottomans, a fact, which give the proclamation a certain legitimacy; the wanton and the extemporaneous stratagem, which suggested where to go following the evacuation and with whom to speak once there, was at hand, and Panagiotis, on the wagon, headed north and west, four months following the exchange with his mother, who roused the notion of voluntary servility, made the thought—I was not drunk enough when I said that—liking quite with fervency the drink in his head, in the exchange, and also the drink in his head, on the wagon heading north and west, four months following the proclamations, all altercations with drink rather the matter.

The quadric party, which was Panagiotis's own—that is, Panagiotis, Santeia, Stefangianopoulou, and Harito, who was Santeia's brother—were in conviviality with the party, which was four parties preceding their own. Panagiotis had visited the young man, who may have been retarded, many a time, the young man named Tassi, who was a striking artist, and who had relayed to Panagiotis, days prior, his intention to start a piece of the procession heading north and west, and come by and see it in three or four days, an invitation, which Panagiotis was accepting, jumping out of his wagon on that fat and disagreeable afternoon, traversing in the rearward twenty-five meters and twice as many steps, the procession traveling in the opposing way of which Panagiotis was walking, with briskness and with intention—Panagiotis was not so much interested in the sketch as much as he was Tassi, who, while silent and meek, was strong in presence and in his characters. Panagiotis, venturing across the tawdry road, apprehended the rear side of the wagon, in which was Tassi, with his right hand, and then swung his left leg up over the step and into the wagon, where Tassi was sketching a sketch, which was quite finished—he was putting a little bit of shade of the right-hand side of the procession, the foreground the view one would receive looking north and west and walking on the right-hand side of the wagon, the procession, the people and the Animalia and the wagons, dwindled and compacted the further one looked into the background, which was the spatial and the corporeal interacting and finding their way into the foreground Tassi was then producing, in contiguity.

Tassi said without turning and without looking up from the sketch, "Kali mera, Pano."

"Kali mera, Tassi. Zografeisis?"

"Yes, I am drawing and the sketch is almost done."

Panagiotis peered into the parchment and saw the charcoal lines, perpendicular, and the haphazard, which was omnipresent and extricated, though they were minimized and containable in the small parchment, on which Tassi was making emboldened essential areas, following the completion of which, he would sign his name. "It is quite accurate and ominous both."

"It is quite the circumstance."

"You could and may well make a lot of money with that artistic tendency you possess."

"Am I supposed to thank you?"

"I suppose not, not if you do not need to make money."

"Exchanging art for money is ingratiating. Isn't it, Panagiotis, the causation of this evacuation?"

"I suppose it is, Tassi."

"I would rather keep my art and let it dry and flake into sand and fragmentate."

"That's your decision, Tassi. Somebody may well value more so your art than you do, however, in which case exchanging your art for money is charitable."

"Charity is something for nothing. One receives when expending nothing, the opposite party has then none of what it necessitates. Selling art is business. One creates and then one sells a piece for money, and that reciprocation is called commodity."

"Art—"

"My art is not a commodity."

"Right, Tassi, right. I meant no ill offense."

"It is no reason to discuss appreciability."

"I would tend to agree, for the sake of agreeability."

"I might make a sketch for you."

"Good."

"Have a good afternoon, Panagiotis, and kali spera."

"Same to you, Tassi, you small and obdurate fruit." Panagiotis then apprehended the handhold with his left hand and stepped down with his right foot and swung back into the procession, traveling in likeness.

Santeia said, "Where did you go?" She had been in the wagon and Panagiotis had not told her he was going to see Tassi and his sketch, and he told her where he had gone and whom he had seen once he returned to the wagon. "Oh," she said. "How is he?"

"Disparaging and frustrated."

"Same as us all."

Panagiotis said, "I am not disparaging, nor am I frustrated."

"What are you?"

"I am not relevant, Santeia, but I will tell you what we are, this procession. We are losing feet."

"We are losing feet."

Panagiotis began to recite: "It is he, Ectognatha, he who licks for the soma of young and the old and the bones and the gold and the nicks of the horse and also the fleece of the ram who is mad and the ram who is gay in the land known as Colchis is good for the hair on your skin is the clock which was thrown in the baby of he, Ectognatha, he who licks for the s—"

"Ennius, shut up. Shut your—"

"—is good for the hair on your skin is the clock which was—"

"Good, good. Keep it up."

Panagiotis did keep it up and would keep it up for many seconds, thinking while in soliloquy, I think she's a virgin—the sun as black as the parallelogram, which illuminated it, the masque behind the black behind the backdrop, which was in lack of perspective in its absolution, and which was as collinear as two flasks of aquaregia, in the apprehension of popularity—the melodious and dichotomous stampeding mounted men en route towards Mesti and in semblance with he, who was Panagiotis, and who had tightened his belt and knew it would not be loosened.

Santeia said, after some hours, during which Panagiotis went to the wagon, which was the winery's wagon, and which had inside of it the remnants of the winery's wine and the last casks of wine having been made in that winery outside of Constantinople, "Stefangianopoulou had better stay out of trouble. It is quite the case what we were talking about earlier. People in villages won't regret killing anybody. He had better keep his composure."

Panagiotis had traded for wine a few utensils for eating and made of silver and also what Panagiotis liked to call geilasma, that is humor, and he returned to hear Santeia with her remark concerning Stefangianopoulou and his stubbornness, to which Panagiotis replied, "Stefangiano-poulou has an objective. Nobody is going to deter him from his objective. The only person who could have is that girl we had mentioned and who has been forgotten by he, Stefangianopoulou, and in good intention. He is going to villages where he knows people, who may well know him. He has his property."

"He has his objectives. He has more than one objective," said Santeia, who was referring to the pentagram of goings on, which Stefangianopoulou and Harito were exacting, a letter to an acquaintance of the father of Stefangianopoulou—the contents of the letter Stefangiano-poulou had declined to discuss upon Santeia's inquiries; he had mentioned a site on one of the hills surrounding Constantinople as a reason for the writing of the letter and did not extrapolate the peculiarities—a stavro of one of the youngest of Santeia and Harito's family who had assumed a place of living further west, and who left most of his belongings in the small town of Kassitera, where the family had their origins; a silver necklace and earrings, which had been of the mother of Santeia and Harito; a small collection of gold, which had been stowed away by the father; and the proscriptions of the father, who had written in Kassitera, and who had died in Kassitera, the proscriptions of the father the per happenstance exemption, or means of escape from the indiscriminant movements of the Ottomans, if they had been read and if they had been enacted—all of which were the representations of corporeal maleficence and perpetuity in not only the few individuals who were incorporated, the individuals who had written and wore and rewritten the effects, but they were also representations of the persistence of life. "You have been quite busy," said Santeia.

"I have been quite busy," said Panagiotis, who was drinking of the bottle of wine. "Would you have a drink?"

"Yes, I would."

"Have a drink," said Panagiotis, who handed her the bottle of wine.

"I would have a drink as a celebration, but I can't because this is not a celebration. I would have a drink as a signal for summons for more drink."

"You fickle thing."

Santeia drank the wine and her eyes got darker. They were already rather dark. Brittle axles and metronomy—the burnoose attired people upon leaving the city, the burqa wrapped girls upon leaving the city, the burro in front of the wagon, pulling the wagon beside the second burro, both of which bolstering the inflammation, the bursitis, which had become manifest in the shoulder and hip of Santeia on this wagon who slept right lateral decubitus—all had thirstied Santeia, who took another shot of the wine, which Panagiotis had apprehended with the cutlery.

"That wine will have you feeling better. Hand it over. I'm only trying to identify."

Santeia returned the bottle of wine into the hand of Panagiotis, and she said, "What of your people?"

Panagiotis said, "I suppose I will have to go out into this lot and find them or stand existing without them. I am not just a standing and immobile person. I could find them in this lot. The question is, in which direction would I follow, north and west or south, in the direction we have come. I may well find them back in the city before I find them here. Pulling on her blouse once I have found her and my mother turning to me, I may well find myself thinking, That's not her." Panagiotis was aware of the wine in his stomach and quite cognizant of the bounding and rebounding polity rising into his thoracic cavity. "I may well go backwards and find myself thinking, What are you doing all the way back here?"

Panagiotis did deliberate with the notion of going in the backwards direction. He did have the idea his people were in the backwards direction in all seriousness. Panagiotis in need of the desirability and the fulfillment of traveling in that direction; Stefangianopoulou and Harito traversing the topography in the opposite direction; and Santeia, sloven and collected, expressing patience in the wagon—all disembodied the universality, which was once an infinite constancy, and which was in diminution, Panagiotis, Stefangianopoulou and Harito, and Santeia a consanguine auger and approaching Eptadendros.

1453

Maudlin, the recurring aspectuls of the city feigned and fluctuated. The borders of the city were in a stretch of exchangeability. It was not uncommon. The residence, which Constantinople had assumed, fluctuated as much as its borders. The city remained in its prescient sustainability. The borders, the name, the significance in polity, and its substantiality many a time found themselves in strange holds and was a tenuous pursuit by both philosophers and tyrants, who were whimsical, and who were famished. The idolatry sustained. The marks on confidence and colloquy were dealt. The people who resided in that city maintained their absolutability. Pantagathus had been awoken, not by the iconoclast callings of priesthood, as was the case most mornings. Pantagathus had not been awoken by the jubilant chortles of the children, but rather, he had been awoken by the silver coin, suspended in the early morning skies, and by the seeming notion, which had descended by its sublime rays—the city in flames and the fragrance of burning eucalyptus, lonesomeness and vermillion licks of hot and piquant flame on his face, the city of Constantinople barren and voided of all, but for the pavement and the works and the walls and high towers of that city in flames, burning and writhing, as an aperture into pandemonium. He had awoken from the otherworld exchange and found himself quite jarred and still feeling the licks of that element on his face and still in the semblance of that burning city, which he quite recognized as Constantinople, and which he contrived would well be sacked; and he went to the small kitchen in his house, which was outside of his bedroom and had a glass of warm water, which settled his tempestuous heart.

He did walk outside into the early morning. The shine piece, the Levanah, was asking of his presence; and he did walk outside, against his intuition, and did not crane his head and did not look either way down his street, but watched the gate, the wooden gate, which separated his property from the public streets and was agreeable in its incombustibility—all was the assuaged morning as was the Constantinople normality—and Pantagathus well conceived it was not going to remain mashoogna.

Pantagathus regarded the planetary compatriot only by its universal casted luminescence; he acknowledged the spaciousness in between the radiance and he, as a constituency in between he and the gods; and he regarded the derivations in the forms of the architecture, which surrounded him, and the foliage, which surrounded him, and the goings on inside of either of the architecture and the foliage, which would well become the torch—How do they do it?—all seeming and consolidated as one manifestation in totality and in danger. Pantagathus regarded the foliage and the architecture and their seeming upholstery, and he regarded the derivations and regarded the gods, and he also regarded the radiant Levanah, and he quite released a tendency, which was of the spirit, and which was quite replaced with the notion he had been having for many a second—it is over—regarding now the forty minutes in all of reality, in between chaos and the stretch of incredulity and the bountiful thing, which was rising in the East, and which he had donned αἰϝών, that is life, but not linear life and not monomomentous life, but rather a comprehensive existence and a polyoptic life, and in consternated schism.

He, this morning, decided not to expedite the morning insofar as his priest duties. This morning had an itinerary— visit the middle-aged woman, who was mourning a lost familial member, and who lived south of his house; and also an old man, who was named Stapo, and who regarded himself as a sort of intelligence in the city of Constantinople, which had been under attack from the east for a few weeks as of this morning. The Ottomans relented at night for their insatiable volition amongst themselves and also to allow the Byzantine forces to move and make strategical mistakes.

As far as the old man, that is Stapo, nobody knew if he were really an intelligent man or only mental deviant. These small chores Pantagathus was to perform prior midday, when he was to convene with other priests and discuss the religious actions and the actions of the church, resulting from the bombardment from the east, Pantagathus also making the intention well in mind to visit hospitals of the sick and hospitals of the ill prior his own evacuation into the hills, which surrounded Constantinople in their heptagram- mic topography. The αἰϝών had arisen in the east. Pantagathus had a breakfast of bread and cheese, upon waking in the early morning, and, upon going back to bed, to lie down for a few minutes, had fallen asleep and had once again been scorched by the heathen flagellations.

He sat, in the front side of his house, with a cup of warm water to settle his tempestuous heart. The chortles of children were heard at this hour, as were the occasional blast of weaponry, which may have been aimed for the walls of Constantinople, but were not aimed at the walls of Constantinople, not yet, but rather, Pantagathus knew, aimed at the navy ships at battle in the Golden Horn, a bay, on the west of which the city of Constantinople had been situated for centuries and ever since the crest of civilized and superior Man—two or three children were at play in the street in front of the house of Pantagathus, who lived alone, and who had, too, lost a familial member, his wife, to unexplainable effects; Pantagathus contrived it was the requests of the gods, but the inflamed eyes told him it was something more along the effects of a massive stroke, and he did not address the notion, nor did he let the body œconomics of the departure register in his mind—Zeno, the boy who lived with his parents alongside Panatagthus's own house, now taking the old lady's stead, as conviviality in the home and as a commandeered associate. The parents of the boy did not consider the boy, Zeno, to be a haughty one, and neither did Pantagathus, who gesticulated Zeno come over to the house on that mid-morning, with a laconic sweep of his hand. Zeno was not haughty. It was true he was getting to the age of rambunctious pursuits, but he enacted nothing to the effect, which neither Pantagathus, nor his parents, would call rancorous, and in all of actuality, it was not a year to be as so, for the gainful and indiscriminant easterners. Pantagathus did gesticulate over the boy, Zeno, and Zeno did come over to the small house, and he walked through the wooden gate, which hours earlier was agreeable in its incombustibility, and which was now agreeable for its give, the boy walking through the gate and sitting down opposite Pantagathus and saying, "Pleasantries, Papa."

"Hi, Zeno," said Pantagathus, the priest, who was quite cognizant of the terminability of the day and, insofar as conversation, what was relevant. "How do you feel this morning?"

"Well, Papa. I feel well. For what more could one ask?"

"Wine and isolation."

"Bafu."

"You don't want to be like that."

"There is no reason to be any one way, not with what is going on outside of the Mesoteichain and in the Golden Horn."

Pantagathus said, "Talk like that and your parent will have a valid reason to talk of you as they now do. Zeno is getting big. Zeno is getting smarter. Zeno is this. Zeno is that. Zeno is the other thing. What are you feeding them to have them talk as so? Or are they feeding you exceptionability?"

"Let's put it this way," Zeno said. "When they call for me, when I'm out here in the sunshine and running around and talking to girls, and when I hear them call my name, it is as if nobody's calling."

Pantagathus said, "Zeno, you—"

"I hear their voices calling and repeating my name, but it is as if nobody's calling, and I go to them anyway."

Pantagathus said, "It's not that bad. It's not that bad, Zeno."

"It won't be that bad once these xilotripes enter my city."

"Constantinople can withstand their bombardment much like their women can withstand my hot piss."

"We will do bath amongst the canines."

The devil, intuited Pantagathus. He is getting rather burlesque. Zeno had arisen from the wooden chair and went back out through the wooden gate, which was agreeable in its incombustibility, and back into the street with the two children, who had carried on in their raillery. Pantagathus would not bathe this morning, not with the water of the cistern, which fed into his small house, nor with the canines. Rather, he would dress and assume his usual person, that is Pantagathus, the priest, and circumvent around the city, making points and stops, hither and yon, descending blessings unto the poor and procuring strength among the weak, and then he was to dine in his small house once more, much in similitude with the meal of the morning—bread and cheese and, of course, a shot of wine—and then, perpetuate in his circumvention, in contiguity. He did look in his box of foodstuffs, prior advancing into the mid-morning. He saw a quarter loaf of bread and a wedge of cheese, and he did also catalogue the days, which were to proceed this day, insofar as sustenance, this morning being his last in Constantinople and full well to his likeness. The bombardment had been ensuing for weeks and the city was going to fall to the Ottomans. Everybody—the priests, who discussed the ramifications of the church in the context of the fall of Constantinople; the children, who discussed chivalric desires and exacted sword fights of wooden blades;

the stall peoples, who apprehended fruits and vegetables and oils from their affiliates in the western part of the city borders, which were now quite exhaustible, and who sold their fruits, vegetables, and oils, and other goods, necklaces and toumbi and flutes and refined pieces from metals to porcelain, to passersby and consumers of all types and of all religions and residence, too, talked of the precocious city in its volatility, all the while pushing, in the midst of cannon fire and shouters, their products with indelibility—and all of whom knew the city were to fall into the huer hands of the Ottomans, and Pantagathus—I'm going to have to find a new place to buy this cheese—was in the discourse of making a terminable circuit around the city, as memorandum of its prescience and also of his priesthood. He was not to pursue the cloth any longer, not after this exchange, and if he were to go ahead and pursue the cloth and go against his instinct, it would not be much different to the church in its entirety, in that the fall of its origins was of importance, which was the reason for his finalistic circuitry. The regalia, however, found its way onto his person this morning, as it did every morning, and Pantagathus found himself in a tenebrous thrill, which resided in his loins. This, his second to final exchange with this house, was at an end, and he went outside into the arisen morning and traversed his way south towards the middle-aged girl, who had lost a familial member, and who was named Theodora.

He did glance at the buildings in their monochromatic constancy. The building had but little changed over the century preceding the year MCDLIII, 1453. Their absolute substantiality played into the undeniable desirability of this city, in the hearts of the Ottomans. They needed nothing more than this city to initiate their temporal and illusory pursuits, which were, now, relevant.

Pantagathus walked into the house of Theodora, not knocking and not so much considering anything else besides the transference of the city and all it represented, religion, morality, justice, and the apprehension of all one couldst desire, into the possession of another body, Theodora sitting at the table in her own kitchen and drinking a cup of water and turning to Pantagathus, stating with fidelity, "Papa, pleasantries. You don't knock anymore, I have noticed. You walk right in to where you please and there are no consequences of it, I am sure."

"You have noticed that, haven't you, Theodora. Pleasantries. The only question is who takes after the other? The body in the east after I, or I after the body in the east?"

"I would have to ask you the question, Who would be the first one to expire?"

"Quite sagacious of you."

"Have you come to console me in this time of consternation?"

"Of course. Of course."

"Sit and have a cup of water."

Pantagathus sat at the table, and, when Theodora put the cup of water on the table, he said, "Thank you, Theodora. What could such a worn out Papa do in your absence?"

"He could exasperate."

"Very good," said Pantagathus, as he took a drink of water. "Are you to be leaving sooner than the idiots enter the city?"

"I have nobody with whom I can leave. I suppose I will escape with the procession of the morrow."

"You will be making a close escape if at all. The shouter I overheard on the way here was saying something about the Mesotheitian falling by this evening."

"I may well end these theatrics like my brother."

"He is gone and his actions are an attractive possibility in this scenario."

"Right. He's dead."

"He's escaped in a bettered way than you and I shall, perhaps."

"What will happen to us? What will happen to the city and the artistry and the iconography? What will happen to Him, O Athanatos?"

"We will be disfigured. The city and the artistry and iconography will be disfigured and will be brought into the possession of the enemy. Athantos will remain in martyrdom and dejected."

"Don't talk like that," said Theodora, falling down onto her knees and crying into the knee of Pantagathus—and down she goes—Theodora repeating, "Don't talk like that. Don't talk like that. Don't talk like that."

"Constant stories are the propellants of honor. You want to get up and sit down on this chair, Theodora, and relay Constantinople in its descendants. Constantinople will precede cities and people, and it will precede constant stories as an invisible flicker. It is to fortify all ideas, making them tolerable."

Theodora had arisen from her knees and sat back down on the chair, and she took a drink of water. She, then, arose from the chair and dabbed her cheeks with a towel from the kitchen countertops. Returned to the chair, she finished her cup of water alongside Pantagathus, who, too, finished his cup of water, and who was honest. He, then, had arisen from his chair, and Theodora, too, did arise from her chair, and Pantagathus kissed her forehead and removed himself from the house of Theodora, knowing it was the last exchange he was to have with the deprecated kakomira.

His circumvention of this morning would take Pantagathus around the tip of the peninsula, on which Constantinople had been situated for centuries, and to the small square, much smaller than one could conceive—it was a garden in all of actuality and not so much a square as it was a rendezvous for the meditative—where Pantagathus would find a man, who was named Stapo, and who was rather particular in his exchanges, that is with whom he had exchanges and what was said in the exchanges, and Pantagathus was well in the categorical thresholds of worthy, to the æsthetic, who was named Stapo, and who was rather particular in his exchanges, that is with whom he needed to speak and what was at hand in the exchanges, and in mentality. Pantagathus entered the small square, or garden, and saw Stapo sitting in the grasses, around which were lichen of all colors around the grasses, and there were lichen spotted inside the grasses, too. Stapo looked up and smiled his incomplete smile—it was not so much an incomplete smile as it was an empty mouth with a couple disparaged teeth inside—and Stapo, the miscreant, said, "Papa, pleasantries. Sit. Sit down with me."

Pantagathus took the empty seat in the square, or garden. "There is a chair here. Why don't you sit on the chair?"

"Well, because."

"Very good. It makes a seat for me."

"How are you fairing in this trying morning?"

"It is not too different outside of the fact it is my last day in my home town."

"You are leaving today, Pantagathus?"

"Indeed, this afternoon, late in the afternoon, I am going up and into the hills with an acquaintance."

"Very well, Pantagathus. Be fast and get to your destination, arriving with the least amount of severity."

"That will be done, Stapo. I am confident in saying that."

"I am glad."

"—and what of you? Are you not leaving this evening, the evening of the fall of this city?"

"I go—you know, Pantagathus, I go where my intention takes me. I have this intention. I have this intention and then there is a tone and I follow the tone and it takes me to where is my intention."

"A lot of good that has done for you," said Pantagathus, regarding this naked person.

"People think I am out of my head. I see it in the faces. You have that face. I can see it in your face."

"I am not making faces."

"Not yet, Papa."

"What do you consider yourself, then, Stapo?"

"There is this fascination in my belly. It is a shine I have. That is me. I consider myself fascination and I consider myself shine."

"I consider myself shackled in this conversation."

"I am glad, Pantagathus. That is why I decide to talk to you."

"People like this city more and more every hundred years, it seems."

"Cities are much like people. If people like you in these places, you are finished."

"I follow, Stapo."

"Then, I will say again I am glad."

"What are you to do once the Ottomans enter the city?"

"Getting the most out of the least amount of expenditures is the goal of all superior œconomics. Did you know that, Pantagathus? What are you to do once the Ottomans enter the city, you ask me. I am to be a systematic device, mean and practical."

Pantagathus said, "I will say pleasantries, in that case, Stapo."

"Pleasantries, Papa." Stapo returned his vision to the grasses and Pantagathus arose from the small chair in the square, or garden, and traversed up the coast of the Golden Horn, that is the east coast of the city of Constantinople, hearing the cannon fire and watching the men in arms walk along the tops of the walls and transferring supplies to the soldiers within the walls, in metronomy. The exchanges with Theodora and Stapo were exchanges, which occurred en route towards the aim of Pantagathus on this day, that is to visit the hospitals and to convene with the priests, in regards to the battle, which was in its due course of action fifty meters on the right-hand side of Pantagathus.

The walls did stretch further, all the way to the northern most part of the city of Constantinople, where the Galata Tower stood erected and vulnerable in this fatalistic day. Panatagthus well knew it was to be the last time he would see the Galata Tower and he well knew also it was to be the last time he would enter the Hagia Sophia, where the conference—it was more so a gathering of sick and expended priests, attempting to retain the bit of holiness which resided in Constantinople and in that building in all its peculiarities—was to be held, and Pantagathus, in stride and traversing the Corisian Gate, in the area further inwards towards the center of the city, an area of stalls and openness, was seized by a woman, who was holding an infant, and who was crying, "Papa, take him. Take him. Look at him. He is a strong boy."

Pantagathus looked at this woman, whom he did not recognize, and who was attempting to bequeath him with her own child and to rid herself of this person, to save him, to save herself the hardship, the heartache, Pantagathus did not know, and said, "Oh, are you going to give me this baby?"

"He is big and he will be bigger and stronger."

"All has descended upon us as is necessary, Kireia. Take this baby and hide until the morrow and leave with the procession. He—"

"He will be better in your hands."

"He is a child and will take better care of himself than I, if what you say is the case."

"Papa, take him."

"Raise him well and escape with your belongings."

"Papa—" said the girl, and Pantagathus was in stride once more, towards the Hagia Sophia, and quite scared of the words and wishes of the girl. He was scared not so much of her words and wishes, but rather what they indicated and what they signified, in the Byzantine people. She was the girl, who would relinquish her child and, in effect, her ancestors. Pantagathus was well frightened at that notion, but not at all demoralized, walking northwards towards the church and listening to the preparations taking place inside of the city walls and around the city walls; he listened to the conversation of a couple of soldiers, who were breaking in the shade, and who were discussing the weakness of the Byzantine defense strategies and the omission of a rather impervious aspect to the battle tidings and, in effect, its outcome, that is gunpowder, of which the Ottomans had much, and they were not frugal in their application of which, and of which they had much at their expense. The Aërial malefactor of years prior, that is the black plague, which had killed over half of the Constantinople citizens, was an ineffectual aberration in the Byzantine discourse, the black plague descending, the black plague killing, and the black plague rising back into the troposphere, from whence the survivors mused it had come, the black plague replaced by the tidal and faceless peoples of the east, which recurred in its aggresivity, and which was now dematerializing the walled villages of the eastern borders of Constantinople, the individuals who comprised that corporeal body, manifesting faces and characters, the individuals who composed that temporal illusion, concocting ideologies and legitimation, and deciding to take, in the next twelve hours, the Theodosian Walls. The optics of the location, the multichromatic integrations of the city—the bread baking in the homes in preparation for the procession outwards and westwards, the white smoke of which rising from the rooftops of houses; the white dress of particular people; the white porcelain being traded for necessities; and the white ropes, apprehended for the effects, which were to be brought with the citizens of Constantinople, in their evacuation on the following morning—all gave the impression of spaciousness. The perspective of the people indicated the severity of that morning, and it was not the perspective of a beneficiary. It was a suggestion of humiliation. The cranial parts of all, and by the indiscriminant blades of the deprecated, were to make contact with the Byzantine grounds and retain cognizance for one second, or thirty of them, or fifteen of them, and maintain the immaculate epoch, which was colloquized of many a maroon ellipse, the number of which, if one were to count them, were being diminished and were becoming even further diminutive, as if one were to do subtraction.

1923

A specimen of what was called in the Greek language choíros, that is a specimen of a pig, was not far upwards from the wagon, inside of which Panagiotis and Santeia were sitting and drinking wine out of the bottle Panagiotis had gathered hours prior the outburst, which had taken place in the pen, which secured the choíros. The choíros screamed and began slamming the side panels of the wagon. The hysterics were heard many meters in either direction, further towards the frontier, which the procession was pursuing, and also meters backwards, in the direction of Constantinople, which was being quite voided. The choíros screamed and squealed, the only specimen as so in the procession, as far as Panagiotis knew, the refugee saying, "Listen to that poor thing." He was referring to the choíros, of course. Everybody was referring to the choíros in the twenty-meter line segment, in either direction. It was rather shrill and abrupt, the screaming and antics of the choíros, and so was the silence, which followed the haphazard, and which was as heavy as the specimen. "They need to put a bullet in the head and clean it up," said Panagiotis. "We would all be better off."

Santeia had not spoken in some minutes. She was enraptured by the effects of the wine. She did speak when

Panagiotis had spoken about the choíros, who had been subject to the apprehensiveness. Santeia said, "You want meat, is all you want. We would all be better off if we were doused in flora."

"I have not seen a petal in days."

"Do you think they have any intentions," Santeia said, "for those who arrive in the villages northward of here?"

"Your standard hospitality is inevitable."

"They have flora in those towns. The flora is made with the intention of being flora and for the æsthetic pleasantness. With luck, the flora will be at a bloom when we arrive."

"That may be the case if the flora were perennials."

"The villagers get flora when we come, or is it we arrive when the flora blooms?"

"Perennials, Santeia. They would have to be perennials."

"They would say, 'That girl, she is flora enough,' if they were not perennials. Besides, perennials are perennials and for good reason."

"The people of the villages would say, 'We would all be better off if this girl stayed in her fucking house.'" A horse and a rider trotted past the wagon, on which Panagiotis and Santeia had been situated. "They would feed us, in any case."

"I would think so."

"There are many people to feed."

"Yes."

"There are going to be people walking up and into their villages, and there are going to be people with unfamiliar faces."

"We all come from the same place. We share facial characters. There is something familiar about everybody. In that way, there are no such thing as unfamiliar faces."

"We all came from the apes. Apes had similar faces, and people are beginning to take on facial characters, which are unlike any before, and which are unfamiliar. Don't lie to me, Santeia."

"We all come from apes. We all come from flora. What is the difference? There is a people, an organized people, waiting for us to arrive."

"It is a superior machine." There was a quarter of the bottle of wine remaining. Panagiotis took a drink from the bottle of wine, and then he offered it to Santeia, who took the bottle of wine and, too, took a drink. The wagon continued onwards, creaking and breaking the silence, in its fluidic passage towards Thrace and further on towards the Drámas Plain.

Panagiotis did want to stay in Constantinople. He did not want to fight. Panagiotis and many others wanted to stay in Constantinople. Not many people wanted to meet the Ottomans at arms and fewer wanted to expend effort to relent a redundant, and for a millennium prior redundant, force. In the stead of fighting, Panagiotis and the others, who wanted to stay, reveled in the finite hours, which were lessening in number, and which were diminutive in appreciation, until the foreign forces evacuated the city of its citizens, that is the European forces, forces of northern and western nations in Europe, evacuated the city of its citizens in order to seize, or terminate the part of the easterners, that is the Ottomans, in the Great War, which, the conquering forces predicted, was quite close to an end, the voided Constantinople the definitive aspect in the bypassed and aggressive part of the Ottomans, in that war, and in entirety.

The citizens of Constantinople, the soldiers of those far nations, who instilled the evacuation of the city, and also the Ottomans, consumed their confidentiality and their severity in the form of vitamins, that is food and drink, Panagiotis, too—take your vitamins—coercing himself to take his shot of wine prior the full day and prior the evacuations, and he even went outside, the day of his leaving his city, and saw the citizens staggered and wanton and lying about for the procession to begin, and remarked, "Everybody is lounging themselves out," talking quite to himself and of affectation to he, to whom he was speaking, in an initiating and moveable start to a long and drabbled pursuit towards all but miniscule personability, and to all but masqued identity, Panagiotis and the citizens of Constantinople, the foreign forces of northern and western Europe and the Ottomans quite indemnified and quite squabbled in their arbitrary dress; Panagiotis stated, once more, to his omnipresent affiliate, "Everybody is lounging themselves out." He added the notion to the repetition, "I'm the only one with my feet on the ground," and it was similar in that afternoon, on the wagon, with Santeia and the quarter bottle of wine remaining—the citizens or former citizens of Constantinople, lying in their wagons or sitting on their belongings, shirts and dresses and stitched sacks, to stop the inflammation—three boys, off to one side of the procession, not fifteen meters north and westward, in relation to the wagon of Panagiotis and Santeia, playing ποδόσφαιρο, that is football, and Panagiotis, having deliberated for only a second, had arisen and had joined the tripartite pursuit, making it a parallelogram.

Returned to the wagon, in which Santeia had been relaxing with her eyes closed, Panagiotis sat and made, in mentality, a distance to the border of Thessaloniki and Chakidiki. The procession, traversing throughout town after town in that pervasive location, was to be noiseless, and yet it was to be a jarred reaction, taking place in the quiet villages of Komotini and Xanthi and Kavala, all of which were, too, a part of the Thessalonian topography, and in sublimity. The sublimity, which had taken hold of the villages, were an apprehensive notion in the minds of Panagiotis, Santeia, and just as well all of the refugees, who were bounded into the mountains of Thessaloniki, and it was as if the villages were illusory fortifications of confidence and shots at retaining their bolstered recalcitrance, which had become too pressurized, and which had bounded into latent deposits of tolerability. The angst and laconic demeanors of those, who were in the undiscovered territories, had begun to have, much like the exiles in actuality, exchanges with attrition and in fidelity, the travelers and the villagers, too, having exchanges with the displacement—Panagiotis quite fastened to the notion, I want to do it when they're asleep—making an entrance and an exit, all of whom incorporated undisturbed in the breakage of borders. "Are you awake?" asked Panagiotis.

"Of course. How could one sleep in this animalistic exhalation?"

"You are an articulate girl."

"I have been to known to speak my mind."

"That's good, as long as you don't let your tongue slip."

"I have been known to articulate, Pano. My tongue doesn't slip. It never has. I can assure you, as far as you're concerned."

"Your tongue hasn't slipped once? Not even once? With a boy back home? Don't lie to yourself."

"My tongue has not slipped."

"Have you had a boyfriend."

"Once, I had a boyfriend."

"Was he a good boyfriend."

"I need him extinguished, and then he would be a good boyfriend, as far as you're concerned."

"Why do you say that? Was he a bad boyfriend? Is that what you are insinuating?"

"He told me once to come over to his house the following morning after my morning chores were done. I went over to his house, which was on the west side of Constantinople. I knocked on the door and he invited me in, and thirty minutes later he was getting all blemished in the face and he told me these words, Panagiotis, and I am not embellishing. He said, 'I am going to slap you in the head with my stick.' That, of course, was following the discussion we had had about making sex, and, I must admit, I was pretty excitable at that point, and then, he talked like that and I was out the door and back in my garden, fifteen minutes later and counting my figs, to see if I could spare one on his blouse."

"Articulation, Santeia, is your benefactor."

"Do you want to know what I did to him afterwards?"

"I'll give you a thousand million United States dollars if you were to tell me."

"I told his father I had found him with a cucumber up his kolotripi."

"Indeed."

"I jest you not. Now, kill me and end this horror."

48

"I would not be the one to kill you. The one to kill you would be the one, who is in this bottle," said Panagiotis, who was holding up the quarter bottle of wine. "But," he said to Santeia. "If it were to be the one to kill you, one would have to mix into it all the colors, and then we could call it one of four names. The decision is yours: (1) Trelos, (2) Koutos, (3) Vlaka, and (4) Paithasmenos."

"I'll decide on the one that tastes best in my falafel."

"Paisthasmenos, it is, then." Panagiotis sat down beside Santeia on her side of the wagon, which was the right -hand side of the wagon, and tapped her knee, and then gave her the bottle of wine, of which she took a long drink. "It's good wine," said Panagiotis.

"It is."

"It won't kill you."

"I know it won't kill me."

"If it were to kill you, it would kill me, too, and then, the monoliths of buildings back home would be well ours to consume."

"For what end?"

"For the taste."

"I hear they have a location in Chalkidiki, called Polygyros. It is in the mountains and it gets cool in the autumn, when it's warm and too warm in Constantinople. That's one end, of which I can find myself a part. I would not mind being killed in a town named Polygyros."

"I would not mind being killed in a town named Polysouvlaki."

"Make it happen. The town is out there."

"The first objective in being killed in a town named as such would be to kill choíros, over there. In that case, we can have much of the sausage."

"I would have to beat him to nekritki akampsa, to make a pristine effect."

"Why would you say that? To have your body harden up is not good, nor is it pristine. I'm not going to remember this upon such an exchange. I need to remember this."

The œsophagus of Panagiotis began to tighten at the topic of nekritiki akampsa. His stomach assumed a dilating poise. He needed more wine as much as he needed to remember this afternoon, not for what had already occurred, but rather for what was to occur, which was a subordinate interaction, his nipples smartening and imploring him to regard his shatterable metatarsals. "The next time I leave this house for an extended period of time is when they take me to the cemetery."

"Who will be the one to take you to the cemetery," said Santeia. "Your wife?"

"My wife? No such thing."

"There is a certain awe in not having somebody."

"Awe—yeah, if you wanted to articulate as so."

"I said that because I wanted to say that," Santeia said, quite aware of the notion she had been having for the latter half of the hour—I'm going to be thinking of this asshole for the rest of my life—and she did not dismiss the notion, but instead held to it fast, as if she were a depredated girl, which was not at all who she was, and both she, Santeia, and Panagiotis knew that well; they noticed it in their arms and in their legs, which had gone lank, and which had begun to feel as if they were structured with hollow bones. Sanetia and Panagiotis regarded their gravitation, which was like plumage, and Santeia—I have had better ideas—and

Panagiotis—she has the tiger's eye—breaching a connexion, the Djinn down and brooding, the Black Sea and the Ægean Sea, both of which were opposite the other and traversable by the Bosporus, cracked and smelted.

"It is a pleasantry we have this cover over us," said Panagiotis, referring to the canvas, which was tied to the four posts of the wagon, on which the two were situated, and the bottle of wine shiny in the refracted sunshine, onto the persons of Panagiotis and Santeia, and the strenuousness straight from Egypt, and the question from Santeia:

"What would you look at, my nakedness or silver?"

Panagiotis's response, "Silver."

"Don't be a fool."

"I am not at all a fool."

"Well, are you the Omega or the Iota?"

"Iota is the most worthless vowel in the alphabet."

Santeia took a drink of the bottle of wine, and then Panagiotis took a drink of the bottle, and then Santeia once more, and then back to its apprehender, and the quarter bottle of wine was only glass in minutes.

2017

The owl pellet, which was elusive, did find itself in the hand of Pete Tsiminis not too long after the Betulaceæ had been vacated of most of the students, who were gathered around the school bus and waiting for the return ride to the elementary school, where they would proceed to dissect the pellets, exposing each of their skeletal subjects for the afternoon. Pete Tsiminis joined them, along with two other students, all of whom had found their peculiar accompaniment for the revels.

The school bus jarred loose any apprehensiveness, with its incohesive mechanics. Pete Tsiminis had been rolling the owl pellet in the palm of his hands, one palm of one hand, and then the palm of the other, and feeling its hairy coarseness and its hardness in them, the school bus traversing over the railroad tracks, each rail and the axle of the school bus predominating, for a second, as a capital H, and as manufactured crosses.

Pete Tsiminis, who was rather deafened by the raillery, which had ensued, conceived the Otus, who was to, per happenstance, create this owl pellet, the innards of which were derivative of an action, which was attributed to survivability, and which was a derivative of a decision, made by natural order, in that the Otus did, and many a time, tie up her babies. Two students on the left-hand side of Pete Tsiminis had been discussing a girl, who had rather seeming eyes, which were green, and which, they said, reminded them of the Otus, or what they perceived as the Otus, because they never saw one in their lives—the student furthest towards the window, "She makes bad choices," and the student closest Pete Tsiminis, who was listening and deliberating taking part in that conversation, "I wouldn't go for a girl who made those choices," the latter student wearing a magenta jacket, which was rather garrulous in the autumnal afternoon, and which was distasteful, it struck Pete Tsiminis, as he sat in his school bus chair—thinking, poor thing—not knowing if he were referring to the magenta student or the skeletal remnants in his hands.

Pete Tsiminis had been working on a particular notion. It was more so a cue, or a mental initiation, which he oriented for himself. It was a series of syllabic enunciation, the words and syllables commixed in an oracular and heptasyllabic commencement—it's going to be melo-dramatic—and Pete Tsiminis, who was quite excitable, and who was expectant in his afternoon, the afternoon during which he was to say the verse, articulated the heptasyllabic inside his head, knowing it had been well contrived and knowing it had been in development for weeks.

The school bus pulled into the roundabout bus loop of the elementary school, and the students deboarded the school bus, systematic. Each had an owl pellet in their hands and few were speaking of the afternoon and its scientific pursuits. They were discussing the spelling of bologna and they were discussing the football field just west of the elementary school and they were discussing the popsicles, which always were found in the cafeteria coolers. Students were silent, too. They traversed the halls of the small elementary school and found themselves, owl pellet in hand, in the science room, with its charcoal tables and blackboard, on which was written in big white letters, Otus, and there was a drawing of the Ornethura beside the terminology; the students took their seats and fell quiet to the demands of the science teacher, who began handing out construction paper, on which the students were to reconstrue their skeletal affiliates; the science teacher, who was the most dismissive person in the faculty—and what a terrible person he was, as was the commonality in the student perspective—handed out KitKat bars along with the construction paper and told the students to begin working on reconstructing their specimens, with care. Two of the students on the right-hand side of Pete had resumed their rubber pencil performance, and Pete Tsiminis took his own pencil and, tight in his hand, began to wave it back and forth, and it looked like a manual fan, one which was expandable and collapsible, and one which had either flora or Ornethura as decorative, which was appropriate. The students, the quiet and the jesters, the science teacher and the drawing of the Otus on the blackboard and the terminology beside the drawing of the Otus, and the charcoal tables and the owl pellets and the indecipherable nonsense, which was carried on in between the students and in between the figure eight items—the posters with anatomy, the models of plant cells, the microscopes and the beakers and the Bunsen burners—all comprised themselves as an incomprehensible glimpse into the ουρανός, which was a constancy in Pete Tsiminis, and which was beginning once again to coalesce, Uranus, the son and the husband of Gaia, who was Mother Earth, having exchanged places with Father Sky, Pete Tsiminis having made his fingers, and reciting *Nive Hucleus Nebulæ* over the owl pellet and breaking it open with two hands to peer inside and find the residual recompense of the Otus envisaged with the skeletal remains of Rodentia, the sustenance of the Ornethura, which was drawn on the blackboard, and which was, the students supposed, in residence within the manifestation, within the Betulaceæ, from whence they had come, a supposition not at all the case and a motivator nonetheless, and once more a *Nive Hucleus Nebulæ* over the reconstrued specimen of a mouse, one which was being examined by a girl, who was rather skinny, and a request by the science teacher for Pete Tsiminis to bring down to the principal's office a small something the dismissive individual had written, of which Pete did not know the first thing, and once arriving in the principal's office a third recitation of *Nive Hucleus Nebulæ* in the direction of the radiator, because it had gotten cold, the principal's gate opening and an entry into an empty conference room, in subsequence.

The conference room, in the chacheés of memories in Pete Tsiminis, began to cremate into otherworld successors, opposite rhombi in a faceless personage, with one body and interconnected and attached to one another, as an organism, which was in collinearity—the face and body as two individuals and the face and body as entwined—the faceless personage lending suggestions to either of the rhombi, the white rhombus or the yellow rhombus, the leaden rhombus or the mahogany rhombus, so it would be good, all sharpness—the rhombi and the collinearity and the faceless personage and the body—all reconstructing themselves in the mind of Pete Tsiminis as high noon, which had stricken ten minutes following the first of the *Nive Hucleus Nebulæ*, and which had sustained in that museum exhibit, with the chalice, which had attracted Pete Tsiminis, hardening in his vision; and, from the people and buildings, who had enlightened their lives with the unchangeable architecture of that city, there were people dancing and burning in the chalice, inciting one another with encouragement—you're sexier than that; you're better than that—enlarged, and they looked so hot. The symmetry of the belly dancer, who had affixed the attention of Pete Tsiminis, had a fifty-fifty countenance, that is one side was as the other, which made either side fifty, and which in affect made one side zero, capable of variability. The notion, as by the suggestibility of her tongue, made fifty-fifty a phantasm. The derivation of the suggestion and the derivation of her tongue birthed mathematics. The suggestibility and tongue, the mathematics and phantasm were lenders to the bimbo, who was substantial, and who was quite the conflagration inside of the chalice and inside of the museum. The eyes of Pete Tsiminis turned towards the clock, which read high noon; and he looked back at the chalice, with the rubies around its base and with the sapphire, and it was still.

1453

Pantagathus made it to the Hagia Sophia at minutes past noon. The meeting was already taking place. Priests and bishops had gathered around a few tables in the communal area. They were discussing many items, the first of which was the conglomerate decision on what to do with Papa T—, who had died in the preceding night, and who was quite strewn in one of the rooms of the Hagia Sophia, awaiting, although with distance, the decision of the priests and bishops.

"Papa T— must be buried this afternoon. There is no time for the typical ceremonies. Family and friends gathering around will have to be content with his burial in Constantinople while it is still ours," one of the priests was saying.

Another priest said, "We must take him and evacuate him with the rest, who manage to leave in this day. Perhaps the morrow is, too, a good time for Papa T— to find his burial place."

A priest had, the morning of the conference between all the priests and all the bishops, harvested his lemons, which came from a tree behind his house, and he was giving them out to priests and bishops, who would accept them. There were many lemons, and there was no possibility of him dispersing of them all. At this point in the conference, at the point in which Pantagathus had arrived, the priest with the lemons had dispersed of twenty-one lemons, and the priest with the lemons arrived at the sitting place of Pantagathus, and the priest with the lemons offered him three lemons, which Pantagathus accepted. He was listening to the conversation regarding Papa T— and did not thank the priest with the lemons, and the priest with the lemons did not care. He was not offended. He, in fact, wanted to thank Pantagathus for accepting the lemons, of which there were many. There was no way he was to disperse of them all, and the priest with the lemons was also implored to put some of the lemons with Papa T—, in his burial place in Constantinople or with the procession, which was sure to leave within a few hours, and which was to take Papa T— with it to a safe location, and in constituency. The conference had begun to talk about Ottoman interactions in Constantinople when the Ottoman forces did enter the city.

"That still leaves the question, what are we to do with Papa T—," said one priest.

Put a layer of honey, and then flip it, and then put a layer of honey. Pantagathus was regarding the haphazard, which was ensuing in the Hagia Sophia, and which had become quite a rancor. Pantagathus was envisioning a gravesite for Papa T—. He noticed the name of Papa T— on the gravestone, and then he regarded the army outside of the walls and quite knew no gravestone would be placed. It was to be an unmarked grave, which made him decide on sending the corpse of Papa T— with the procession this evening and giving him a ceremonial burial. The priests and bishops did vote on the issue, the decision of which was to send Papa T— along with the citizens of Constantinople and a young priest, who had voted in favor of the evacuation possibility. The young priest did not want to leave the city; he had made this known. The conference was becoming such a rancor that, in fact, the young priest decided to take the corpse and take it west to quell the harangue.

"Thank you, Papa S—" said one bishop.

"After all that, now you're going to thank me," said the young priest, who was rather disconcerted. Everybody could see it. "What are we going to do upon the Ottomans entering the city, is the more important question."

"There are three options," said the bishop, who had addressed him. "One, pay the jizzya. Two, convert. Or three, fight." The priests and bishops began once more in their raucous. "It does not give me happiness to say it, but those are our three possibilities."

"We are not paying the jizzya. The Ottomans will take everything as it is. We are not to convert. The Ottomans will enslave us to a deepened degree."

"Do you propose we fight? Do you suppose we fight like the soldiers?"

"Of course."

"Those who want to fight will fight," said a second bishop. "Those who do not want to fight can stay in the Hagia Sophia and attempt to coerce the eastern forces out of their volition. It will not be pretty. The people are scared."

Pantagathus said, "It is a good job the people are selfless."

"You are correct about that, Pantagathus."

"I will go into the hills this evening," said Pantagathus. "It will be dark, but not so dark, and the twilight will aid my passage. All are to accompany. The city will fall today. I have had a dream."

"I have had this dream," said a priest.

"I, too, have had this dream," said another priest.

"I have had this dream," said another priest.

"I, too," said a bishop.

"This is the case and in totality. It has been determined. All who want to go with Pantagathus into the hills may go into the hills with he." A man, who was not a priest, came into the meeting and dispersed of bread; he then brought wine for the priests and bishops.

When the man, who was not a priest removed himself from the conference, a different priest said, "What are we to do? Arm the people, who confront us with the fearsomeness?"

"We must arm them with the words, with which to confront the attackers. It may prevent unnecessary death in the church."

Pantagathus felt his own words become callus. They were not the words, which the Ottomans would understand. Even if they could understand the language, the decision would be made to ignore requests and suggestions. The Byzantine and the Ottoman tongues were different, and they were not different in only communicable and superficial ways. They were different in their fundaments.

Pantagathus was to reconnoiter with an old acquaintance, who was named Tavis, the heretic, in the hills.

Tavis, the heretic, had, five or ten years prior, been forced out of the city of Constantinople at the accusation of unorthodox practices. In fact, the practices were quite Orthodox. The priests and bishops, and not as many as were in attendance today, decided on sending Tavis, the heretic, into the hills, where he would stay for the duration. After all the dawdling, all there was left was Orthodox practices, and the suggestion of such a redolent idea only fortified the few priests' and bishops' decision to send Tavis, the heretic, into the hills, where Pantagathus was to go this evening, and where the small home of Tavis, the heretic, was located, amongst the Sciuridæ and the deciduous trees. It had rained on the night Tavis, the heretic, removed himself from the city, and it was not a hard rain. It was only a light and disparaged fall, which adhered to the skin of the priests, who had seen off Tavis, the heretic, Pantagathus one of those priests, who had seen off Tavis, the heretic, and who had voted in the decision of his residence in the city walls. Pantagathus had inquired on the so called unorthodox practices of Tavis, the heretic, and Tavis, the heretic, replied in a redoubtable voice, "It's an illusion," and four days later, the party was standing in the rain, watching Tavis, this heretic, leave the city of Constantinople, through the Golden Gate. Pantagathus mused if any of the priests would accompany him into the hills, where the house of Tavis, the heretic, was located, and autosuggested to himself that none of the priests, nor any of the bishops, were to accompany him into the hills outside of the city walls, which he would escape within the next few hours—they had families and they had to address matters, which were at hand. Exposed below the regalia of one priest, on the right-hand side of Pantagathus, was the shin of a hairy leg, over which was another shin of another hairy leg, and both hairy legs were folded into the other, above the hairy ankles.

The sunshine was coming into the communal room, where the priests and bishops were collected. The window in the small communal room was not a stained-glass window, and there were dust motes suspended in the small area, looking like snowfall in a clear, winter day, the sunshine illuminating the city and the dust motes.

The sunshine had done this during a particular snowfall, too, twenty or so years prior, in the city of Constantinople. Pantagathus had been a child. The city of Constantinople in the midst of a snowfall was a rarity, and Pantagathus had seen snow only once, and he remembered it with clarity—stepping outside of his house, which was further centric in regards to the city of Constantinople than his house now was, and opening his mouth and receiving a snowflake in his mouth, where it dematerialized, and remarking, O how they take your mouth, the snow of that childhood exchange becoming the words of the people, the iambic trimeter, O how they take your mouth, becoming the trochaic, People are a problem, Pantagathus quite renascent and Pantagathus quite steadfast. The snow had a chance to ground itself in the hills. It had a good chance to ground itself in the hills, but not so well a chance in the congested streets of Constantinople, where hither was yon, and where up here was down beneath the paved roads and the dirt roads of the city, Constantinople, which was bound to fall in hours; the city had suggested, I am your daddy, which was changed and received as, Your eye dead diem. Living in the hills with Tavis, the heretic, in his small house, which was made of wood, was to be much different than the miasmic life in Constantinople. In Constantinople, individuals were to give honor to the buildings and the artwork and the individuals in proximity, and individuals were to take it away, without reprehension, and then individuals were to get one of that which was most desired, that is universality in the form of foodstuffs and in the form of fabrics, refined or not it made little difference, the individual getting its sustenance, one after the other individual, receiving abundance of this and incredulous amounts of that, finding oneself remarking—is this all tomatoes?—making remarks on the facsimile effort expended and the fruit, which was in subsequence; Pantagathus quite in the discontented sphere of perspective—his life to be lived in the hills, with Tavis, the heretic, until he decided where else to arrive, and also the logs of distinguishability, which were to enclose him in those evenings in the hills when it was raining, like the evening Tavis, the heretic, had made his exit from the city of Constantinople years prior, and when it was dark—the declaration made, which was to differentiate one seeming second from the next distinguished one, You come here to down Lord Fistikiasas.

The meeting of the priests and bishops did adjourn with pleasantness, and conviviality was prevalent upon the adjourned meeting. The conference was to be the one of the last held in the Hagia Sophia, and it was to be one of the terminal meetings held by religious affiliates in the city as it was then known as Constantinople. The adjourned meeting was carried out into the afternoon humidity, the sounds of the cannon fire audible in the western and eastern expanses of Byzantion—that took some work, the priests and the bishops bidding one another goodbyes, with the honor and with the coal becoming manifest in their metacarpals, the priests and bishops having and enunciating that peculiar basso, which was omnipresent in those peoples, who donned themselves religious, and who donned themselves Byzantine. Pantagathus was to embark on the walk back to his home, which was south of the Hagia Sophia, as was most of the city of Constantinople, and he had already noticed the stalls and the marketplaces of Constantinople, on the walk home, had thinned and were filled with fewer people, the inevitable forces quite close and quite baroque, everybody knew; and the dwindling in number signs of shops and of stall keepers was, too, a lessening reality, in that they might reestablish their businesses in Bavaria and Iberia. Those were the people, who could have made an effort, mused the sauntering Pantagathus; they have in the former years of this empire and they don't help anything in its time of desperateness, referring to the Bavarians. The seeming and peripheral glances of Pantagathus, who looked here and examined there, all the while passing through the emptied streets of Constantinople, assumed their familiar parallelogram cue, his house, with its small windows and wooden gate, which was agreeable as to its incombustibility, and he was in through the door and in his kitchen, where he gathered his quarter loaf of bread and his cheese and a jug of water, donning a close to the house, because it was about to get worse and not a little worse. It was about to get much worse.

1923

It was the canvas overhead which sheltered Panagiotis and Santeia. The outside of the wagon was open and exposed, the sunshine permitted into the wagon, oblique. The choíros had not made a sound, nor had it made a jarred movement in the recent fifteen minutes, during which Panagiotis had apprehended a distaste for his T-shirt. His head had begun to circle through the eyes of Santeia, and then to the shoulder of Santeia, and then to the hands of Santeia, and then to her ankles and back to her eyes, which had assumed a tertiary darkness, inside of their own cotton apprehensions. It did make shelter, that canvas, and for a reason, which was good and colloquial, the procession composed of so many people, who had begun to traverse west through the mountains of Byzantion, which was ephemeral, and who had transmuted into sensibilities, which were, to them, as of that afternoon, incomprehensible—the shattered choíros; the glass bottle, which had been full of wine, and which had been depleted by Panagiotis and Santeia; Panagiotis and Santeia hurrying into nakedness; and the incompleteness of the fascinating strata, on which they traversed—all sovereign and all in contribution to the acrostic that happened.

The preceding ninety minutes and the succeeding ninety minutes, like the preceding ninety years and the succeeding ninety years of that mobile exchange, were a ninety to a ninety degree angle, Byzantion and its dead balls and soap wafers, respectively, which belonged to the citizens, and which were appropriate. It had been a period of tolerability, and the ninety and the ninety were fitted. The two wagon travelers, Panagiotis and Santeia, quite parabolic, Panagiotis—This girl wants to be tits—and Santeia—crying from her fogging pity—the leaden axes of Precambria, and Panagiotis—Suck on my bricks—regarding the Ottoman forces, and Santeia—tralalalalala—because in twenty-four hours, everybody would know which was better, the girl, Santeia, needing to become a nocturnal inclination, and Panagiotis a progenitor to accumulated pieces of detritus, the two, the ninety and the ninety, the dead balls and the soap wafers, and the leaden axes of Precambria—tralalalalala—becoming transparent angles and becoming inverted as two bells, cloyed to one another and within one another, with the reactions and the vibrations; the distal ends of that parabola shaded limits of iron displacing water displacing breasts, which were aquatic and whetted, and which were maritime in their glistened and borderless wanton, the weight in the middle and Santeia tucking her knees on either side of the coxal bone of Panagiotis, the ilium and the ischium and the pubic bones, which comprised his steadfast reciprocation as quite the farce; Santeia, with exactitude, extolled the Pythagorean Theorem and popped a diddly squat on his bimbley dinwiddle—a thin bolt of cotton unraveled and had arisen into thoracic cavity.

1453

The navy, east of the house of Pantagathus, was getting into formation. Pantagathus was sitting in a chair, in the small living quarters. His fat hands had clutched in them his bag, which was full of items—the quarter loaf of bread, two bottles of wine, and the cheese, and there were also three priest blouses and a pair of socks and a pair of shoes, which he was to wear upon work in the hills, living with Tavis, the heretic, and there was also a brush and soap in the bag, which he clutched in his hands—Pantagathus, in a quiet stretch, reveling in the enjoyability of his home, which was to be his home for another thirty or forty-five seconds. He massaged his hands. The evening had descended. The people of Constantinople were gathered in the Hagia Sophia, for the final ceremony, which was to take place in Christian Constantinople. Pantagathus had walked outside of his house, and he walked out onto the hard surface of the Constantinople ground and through the wooden gate, which was agreeable in its incombustibility, traveling west towards the Blanchernæ Walls, in the west on Constantinople, and through those walls, he was to go out and into the wood of Byzantion, through the forces, which were attacking, and through a small area, he knew, was unoccupied. He did walk west, with his bag, and he found the passage for which he had been searching, through the Blanchernæ Walls and out onto the crust of deprecated Byzantion.

He had been walking through the verdant wood of western Constantinople limits for an hour and saw the Ornethura and the Scuiridæ. They were performing the act they had been performing for millennia, to jump out and in front of a seeming individual, who, this time, was Pantagathus, for the individual to constrict his eyes and glance at the nimble specimen, who did not know danger from mpiskota.

Pantagathus approached a churned swatch of ground. Many hoof prints of, per happenstance, two or three specimens Equus caballus were evident. The day light had turned to the thick ambience, which descended on Constantinople evenings, and it had begun to thicken into night, before it would open up again into luminescence. On most nights, Pantagathus enjoyed the darkness, which was found in ill lit stretches of the city, and which was quite omnipresent in the wood west of the city of Constantinople; but the night of importance, which was the night Pantagathus found himself bypassing a churned swatch of soil, was to be piquant and in five or six hours, with the Ottomans attacking the Mesoteichain wall in the middle of the city from the east and the Myroandrion Wall to the north of the city of Constantinople, after which the heinous would enter through the Corisian Gate and round up heads of livestock and horses—someone's or another, cantering through the streets of Constantinople and drinking beer.

Pantagathus reached a clearing, within which were patches of tall grasses. Across the clearing, which was about forty meters in diameter, the wood began once more, with its gnarled foliage and with the thick epidermal of the trees. In the center of the clearing were three people, who were mounted on three specimens of Equus caballus, and who, Pantagathus fathomed, created the churned swatch of soil, two hundred meters and about five minutes behind him. He did stay in the tree line, which was preternatural enough. It did cover him from the eyes of those riders. Pantagathus ensued with a peculiar indecisiveness. The tall grasses were tall and heavy enough to grant protection from their eyes. The chroma of the evening had descended, and that, too, fortified the confidence, which was reasserting itself, in Pantagathus. The three mounted riders had a light. They were in the apprehension of one fire, and they were smoking, Pantagathus could well see, three small ellipses igniting at the inhalation of each of the three riders. The indecisiveness had once more crept into the ribs of Pantagathus, and he did look at the nearest cluster of tall grasses, and once more looked at the tripartite luminary. Confidence, once more, inflated his loins, and with a three count—One, two, three, four—Pantagathus ran, crouched, with his bag of foodstuffs and clothing and supplements, towards the first cluster of tall grasses, and he arrived amidst the grasses, with the pollen and with the cicadas. He glanced at the tripartition—They have not seen me; they are constructed like that—and he regarded the cluster of tall grasses, which was ten meters away, in front of him and closer the opposite end of the preternatural woods—They know nothing—and the jump to the next cluster of grasses, upon entering which, Pantagathus heard the baritone calls of one of the riders. Pantagathus turned and regarded the tripartite mounted men, who had discarded their smokes, and who were in pursuit of the priest, Pantagathus, dressed in black, and who regarded himself, only three seconds ago, unthreatened. The contrary was quite the case, the three horse riders now four mounted men, one having decided to partake in the pursuit, from the edge of the woods. Pantagathus, with his bag, which was heavier than he needed it to be, made chase for the edge of the woods, and saw in his left periphery a geometrical construction, a barn at the peripheral edge of the wood, and he redirected his steps and made chase for the building. The small barn was thirty meters off to the left-hand side of the unaltered course Pantagathus was to take, if the mounted riders, with their smoke and with their numbers, had not been the matter. They were, in fact, and became quite more so the matter every hastened step Pantagathus took towards the barn, which was nearer, and which was a haven within thirty seconds of the original and baritone call; the barn was darker than the night had become on the outside. Bales of hay were stacked in one corner and wheat was piled in the corner closest Pantagathus, on his right-hand side, and in he jumped, into that pile of wheat, which was quite substantial, and which was able to contain his body in entirety, Pantagathus breathing and with heaviness—I've got to stop—and the horsemen now footmen and inside the barn, the breathing having slowed and the percussive hits, which were audible to Pantagathus only, having swelled in his thoracic cavity. The pile of wheat was against the wooden wall of the barn. Pantagathus could hear the breathing of the four Ottomans. Pantagathus was uncomfortable and would reposition himself in eight more beats of his heart. His scapulæ decided to lean back of their own accord. Oh, shit. The boots of the pursuers and the gangly metalloids were loud. One chime rang close to the pile of wheat. The quadric party, who was in search of the priest, Pantagathus, retreated back into the evening. The dense confidence accumulated back inside of the loins of Pantagathus, and then it just fell apart.

The Great Palace had been taken. Northern most buildings were an aspect at hand for the Ottomans, who had entered the city, not long after midnight. Traveling southwards, the pansophic perceived a belly dancer performing in her lonesomeness, while the Hagia Sophia was being hacked of its marbles; an old man eating a fraule, at his kitchen table; Zeno, the young man, with whom Pantagathus had become quite acquainted, deliberating the amount of soiled plasma he had seen in the streets as a chequer of belief or as an illusion, during one stretch of inquisitiveness and bravery when he went outside of his house to see; the Ottoman forces sweeping the tip of the peninsula, on which Constantinople had been situated, and cleaning out houses and abdominal cavities at a whim; the hospitals Pantagathus had visited late in the morning burned and collapsible; Theodora in her home, at her kitchen table with a cup of water and in need of a residence closer to her brother, who was well in circumscription with the Golden Horn, which was a buoyant and splintered barrel of chum—

the tactical preserves of Byzantion quite exhaustible and the Church of Holy Apostles being chopped, in the Petra District—Pantagathus in the home of Tavis, the heretic, at the point of the takeover and in range of the sounds of the disparaged cannon blasts, which ensued until after midnight—That is the most ignorant thing I have ever heard in my life—with the harlots and Stapos now ensconced and with the bodies of Ottomans collected at the walls.

Tavis, the heretic, was speaking to himself. "Je tu Trois. Je tu inflexion. Je tu le cirque. Je ne suis pas Capetien." He turned to Pantagathus and said, "There is money under that sack." He gesticulated towards a sack in the corner of the house. "Geraldo likes the feeling." He gesticulated now to a raccoon, who resided in the house.

"It is better than hay."

"I am allergic to hay."

The Ottomans had congested the outlet, from which Pantagathus had come from the city of Constantinople, the outlet the Kolliomene Gate, out into Kosmidion, where he and Tavis, the heretic, were now discussing weaknesses. The archers were jumping off of the Myriandrion. "What is it for?" said Pantagathus, he now gesticulating across the room, towards the horn of ibis, which had been engraved, and which was porous by design.

"It is to open the Golden Gate."

"Do you jest?"

"Of course, I jest."

"Are you aware of your raillery?"

"Pantagathus, it is good to hear you are as matter of fact as you were when I last saw you upon my exit at the Golden Gate."

"I have retained a certain impressionability."

"As have we all," said Tavis, the heretic, who was quite correct in his response. The only withheld notion, in between the two, Pantagathus and Tavis, the heretic, was that the item, which had been retained, was a dejected impressionability, viz. the divulgent. The Byzantine and the Ottomans had made the decision, while sovereign, to plow westwards.

Pantagathus had gotten up from his chair and went to his bag of belongings. He had noted the wear the body of Tavis, the heretic, had taken since his ousting from Constantinople and it was not too unbearable to the eye. In the nose, it was a little bit different, and Pantagathus let register that the body was to accumulate matter on its person and that the stream, just north of the house of Tavis, the heretic, was the only source of cleanliness, and also that the soap he had brought with him from Constantinople was the only soap in the small house of Tavis, the heretic, and may well have been the first bars of soap to enter this house in years and maybe even since its homecoming. Pantagathus removed the soap from the bag of belongings—I'm just going to put this in here—and deposited the soap into the bottom of the kitchen drawers, where he could find them when they were necessary.

Tavis, the heretic, said, "Let's go outside in the front of the house."

Pantagathus followed Tavis, the heretic, outside in the front of the house. The cannon fire had ceased. Kosmidion had become quite still. The autumnal winds had moved into the region. It was an air unlike any Pantagathus and Tavis, the heretic, had ever smelled, the autumnal air high and agreeable and with the scents of soot and fire, which were even higher in the polity of the evening, and which had descended into the hills of Kosmidion, with vigor. "I noticed the instrument in your quarters."

"I never liked the guitar."

"Do you play?"

"Of course, I do."

"Where did you apprehend the guitar?"

"There is a man, north of here, who has many. I travelled to his homestead and apprehended the guitar there from him some years ago, with the intention."

"It was a good decision, if you have maintained relations with the man from the north, in these kinds of scenarios."

"Yes, it is a good decision for that matter. I had been searching for a mint patch, which I have heard was in the north of Kosmidion, and I came across the homestead. The man was outside, tending his things. He invited me in and I saw the guitars—"

"A builder."

"—and he suggested I take one, a suggestion which I declined, and I thought about it for many weeks and decided I would go to the homestead and examine a worn guitar that had caught my eye, the guitar inside, and he did have to coerce me to take up the instrument—I think he wanted somebody with whom to play—and then I picked up the guitar."

"Do you play?"

"We have played."

"Playing with another would be much different, I can imagine."

The strings were assumed in that evening, and the marble which comprised Constantinople and the stones which comprised Constantinople may well have been dematerialized by that chord, which had been struck by the haphazard, for an expedited quarter note, the shards of walls and the granularity of the ground and the feigning sky all verged into Tzedeq.

2017

The flight back to Newfoundland and Labrador was departing hours after high noon had stricken in the museum exhibit full of Byzantine works. Pete Tsiminis did enjoy his stay in the city. It was quite pleasant. He had even escaped without a blemish, which may well have been received from any bypassing stroller or in the congested train station the family had been frequenting over the past seven days; and he had escaped, too, with haughtiness and certain peculiarities—a poster from the Museum of Modern Art, a metallic apple, and a brass spoon from an antiquity dealer, which the parents of Pete Tsiminis had wanted to visit—and found himself on the T train, mid-examination of one man and his flat nose. Of course, Pete Tsiminis had worn his spoon. Per happenstance, the man with the flat nose would have difficulties, but that was why they had hats. If I had a hat it would be my problem; I don't have any hats, the boy having assumed that lick of haughtiness, and with sarcasm, in anticipation of home in Red Bay, Newfoundland and underarm antiperspirant.

The subway, in which the family of Pete Tsiminis and Pete Tsiminis himself found themselves, was a particular exchange; the subway encapsulated its residents and had a verbosity, which was subtle—It's all me—and which was literature. I don't like it, regarded Pete Tsiminis, and regarding the patchy, incomplete, and porous advertisements and semblance and people, and also regarding a tart taste in his mouth. Their stop was approaching, and then the family of Pete Tsiminis would deboard the T train and head north towards LaGuardia Airport, from where they would bound towards home. The T train squealed; and Pete Tsiminis expended one staccato laugh, along with the centripetal forces and along with the viscous voice, which came from the speakers. The belly of the young Pete Tsiminis fruated, before the contractions.

Airborne, for forty-five minutes, and then in an ovular exchange, Pete Tsiminis looked into the cockpit of the small two-engine aircraft, and he thanked the pilots. The family was on the ground of Newfoundland and Labrador, with the supple evening time climate and with the luminescences. The evening had descended, into its fructuous and Newfoundlander agreeability. The sunshine, which bowed over the curvature, enveloped the airport and the family and, of course, the country, in serendipity—the Sciuridæ, in pursuit of the other for baby, and the footsteps—Pete Tsiminis, in the backseat of the car, which had arrived them in the airport a week prior, and which had been in the long-term parking lot for the week, found with its shine.

Antibodies and disease, paint and directions, and metal and slashes, all were their opposites, and they were all rather outstanding, in Pete Tsiminis, and they were dissociated in their bonds. The mother of Pete Tsiminis was in mid-sentence, saying about speed trains, "It all makes sense, at first, and then I had examined the mechanics and noticed they're backwards." The house, in Red Bay, Newfoundland, was not far away from the airport. The family of Pete Tsiminis arrived home within two hours of the arrival of the plane, and with vigor the father had unloaded the automobile of all the luggage the family had brought with them to the city, and then went outside in the back of the house, where there was a large patio made of mahogany, and where there were chairs made of mahogany, to sit down for a smoke, with the girl, who had been talking about speed trains, too, in a chair, and with Pete Tsiminis also sitting in a mahogany chair and looking out into the wood on the opposite side of their grass and hearing in his left ear the father, who was smoking, and who was boasting about the decision to visit the city, because it had been so many years, and with placidity.

It was minutes before he decided to make a move, Pete Tsiminis rising from his mahogany chair and caressing the wooden piece, like he always did, on the way back inside of the house, with the chisel and with the hammer beside the wooden piece; the patio door was open, and the father, who was done smoking, called inside the house and told Pete Tsiminis to grab an apple from the countertops and bring it over, which Pete Tsiminis did do, with a swipe and, into the lap of his old man, with a lob. The neighbor, who was named Jonathan, and who had spoken of his desires to go to New York City, was to come here, oblivious, tomorrow, to be reacquainted and to be troublemakers.

It was a normality—Jonathan was to use the front door of his own accord. He was to walk right in and say hello to

Mr. and Mrs. Tsiminis, and find Pete somewhere in the house under the direction of Mr. or Mrs. Tsiminis, if Pete was not in the kitchen or in the living room with Mr. or Mrs. Tsiminis when Jonathan walked right in the house, as if it were a home publicæ, which was not too separated from the actuality of the household—spacious and accessible, in all hours of the day and even in a few early hours of the night, when the house was still unlocked in the front door. Pete Tsiminis was in anticipation of a day of hikes and raillery. Pete Tsiminis and Jonathon did agree quite with wonder, and the agedness of the country, which had arched back into modernism, was, too, agreeable to the duo. The cacheés of cold water in the Newfoundland and Labrador winters and the gnarled wood, which creaked, had been replaced with the fœtid solution of selenium and with the nails of cyanide, on which people rested while in repose, and which had become, like the antibodies and disease, and the paint and the directions, and the metal and the slashes, outstanding and imperceptible—people in number who wanted to apprehend the notion to seize the opportunity to snag the chance to hit red monkey in my living room, the country of Newfoundland and Labrador, in Red Bay—Mr. Tsiminis, escaping his suspenders in the master bedroom, and Mrs. Tsiminis, assuming her nightgown only to escape it within the hour, and Pete Tsiminis, in his own bedroom, which was one of six in the house, and placing his poster from the Museum of Modern Art on the vacant spot on the wall and the metallic apple on his nightstand and the brass spoon inside of the drawer in the same nightstand, slumberous and invalid, within two hours.

The windows turned into drapery, and the ceramic vases and bowls became tapestries, and the countertops and the cabinets and the mahogany chairs outside became hammocks, and the Smith and Wesson, which never got any use, in the armoire of Mr. Tsiminis, turned into a slingshot—the chips, which comprised the people of the past seven days in New York City, rotated one-hundred and eighty degrees upwards, and were tiles of a different placement—Pete Tsiminis, who had remarked upon the haphazard, These people don't care, and Mr. and Mrs. Tsiminis quite illustrious, in Mr. Singh's, who, Pete had said, "Given the flavor of this beef... must snivel when he sings."

Pete Tsiminis hit the copper shot, after which he went into the shower, and washed his body with his wife. In actuality, the wood outside of the house was vacant. The shower had inside of it Pete Tsiminis and only Pete Tsiminis. He escaped the shower. The trees, outside of the windowpane, with the reconstrued and skeletal mouse on the window sill, perpetuated in their scleromorphic contiguity. Pete Tsiminis went to the window dressed. He did look out of the window and he saw the sack of firewood. On the windowsill was the reconstrued and skeletal mouse; and he looked at that, too; the s'mores of the prior winter surfaced and the elusive Ornethura, that is the Otus, did seize his eyes, and it was only in his mind—she did that a long time ago—and then, a glance at the Rodentia, which was well glued to a plaque. The old nut was still out there, in the Betulaceæ, where Pete Tsiminis found himself with frequency, and where Pete Tsiminis gauged how fast he wanted his feet to set to a skiptoumolou.

2017

It was the week after Thanksgiving, when Pete Tsiminis went back to school, the month being November, and the morning, of that Monday, was vaporous. The students and the teachers held no substantiality. It was as if Pete Tsiminis could walk throughout anybody and anything—the girl, to whom he always nodded, on the way to science class; the fern, in the middle of the yard, in the middle school; and Jonathon, who was always quite near; and also the teachers and the documents they handed out and the pencils and pens, all seeming and, while insubstantial, confrontable and relevant.

Pete Tsiminis had been taken out of school the week prior, which was the week of Thanksgiving. His parents had taken him to New York City, on Saturday, and straight through the Thanksgiving week, they stayed in New York City, until the following Saturday, when Pete Tsiminis lobbed the apple into the lap of his father, and when the latter had had a smoke, on the patio, with the mahogany chairs and with the symmetry. The middle school, which Pete Tsiminis attended, was a middle school of ordinary size and of ordinary merits. The school did not achieve higher recognition, and it was as if the students of the small middle school in Newfoundland and Labrador were quite wanton and illusory, much like the topography of that country, which was verdant, and which was a candid illogic. The day, that is the school day, had been coming to a close, the students awaiting the cue to go out and into the hallways and gather their effects, and then off in whichever direction towards home and towards milk and whole grain chips. Jonathon accompanied Pete Tsiminis on the walk home. It was not a long walk, not a long walk at all. One went eastwards, towards the fork in the road, following the release of school, and took the right-hand prong, and then x amount of meters later and about fifteen minutes later, one arrived in the street, called Piccadilly Street, off of which on turned to the left and onto Basalt Road, twenty meters down which the houses of Pete Tsiminis and Jonathon were located, in a parallel to one another, with the like Ligustrum, in between the two of the houses. A small boy, who was named Cletus Stein, and who was a meek boy, too, accompanied Pete Tsiminis, on the walk towards Basalt Road, and walked straight forward on Piccadilly Street rather than making the left-hand turn down the road, on which Pete Tsiminis and Jonathon lived.

Today was a day, which was a single hue different than the other days, which preceded this day. Today was the day Pete Tsiminis had, in his pocket, four dollars, and the day it had dropped in temperature far enough to legitimate the suggestion Pete Tsiminis had made that morning, and that was s'mores in the evening time, a suggestion, which had brought him together with the four dollars in his pocket, for marshmallows after school was released. Jonathon had also a ten-dollar bill in his pocket, the two, on the morning following the homecoming after the New York City pursuit, coordinating the inquisition of monies to apprehend the ingredients for the precocious cavort—s'mores and not in lonesome; the parents of Jonathon and, of course, Jonathon himself, were to come over to the backyard grasses of the Tsiminis household and blacken their marshmallows and conceive the wondrous sandwich. It was all really very exciting.

The eastward fork in the road was nearer. Pete Tsiminis and Jonathon had been walking towards the Piccadilly Street for five minutes. On the way to the fork in the road, a hill of mediocre size resided on the left-hand side of the road, on which Pete Tsiminis and Jonathon were walking; it was a sort of hangout spot for the students of the middle school who were not students in that hill, but were more so explorers and scientists and æronautical personnel and orthopedists, speeding down the hill when it was covered with white powder and, on sleds, saw no difference between the coastlines of Newfoundland and Labrador and the 20x microscope lens and aluminized Mylar and bones beside the snow, which was the **oυρανός,** and which was reconstructed at the bottom of the hill, in the dawdle of the children, who had hit the divot at the bottom of the hill, and who were propelled into the ditch at the bottom of the hill where they were to dance and then brush off the fractals.

Pete Tsiminis was to call in the snow, within two weeks. It was to fall and coat the greens of the hill, in entirety. The compatriots of the middle school were to be glad, of course, and they would hit the hill alongside he, Pete

Tsiminis, and Jonathon, in equanimity. The snow was to be called in like the monies, which had found residence in the hand Pete Tsiminis that morning, and which was now in his pocket, with the lint and with the landscape he had drawn in art class, because he needed to show his mother the feet of this moose.

Eastward of the fork in the road, which they had taken, was the Coleman's, where Pete Tsiminis, Jonathon, and Cletus Stein were to pick up the marshmallows with the four dollars of Pete Tsiminis and cinnamon graham crackers with the ten dollars of Jonathon; Cletus Stein accompanied the consumers, for the humorousness, which took place in between them, "I like my marshmallows sticky," said Jonathon.

You like your marshmallows sticky?" said Pete Tsiminis.

"Yes, I like my marshmallows sticky."

"Watch your fingers. They get hot," said Pete Tsiminis.

"I'm always careful with my marshmallows when they're sticky," said Jonathon.

"Watch your ass," said Pete Tsiminis, and then one hundred and twenty seconds later, the three middle school students, who were now Coleman's most diabolical customers, found their way into the snacks and cracker aisles, in search of marshmallows and of cinnamon graham crackers. Pete Tsiminis did find the marshmallows, with ease. There were the small marshmallows. There were the medium sized marshmallows; and there were the large marshmallows, which Pete Tsiminis did not regret picking up.

Jonathon said, "I always liked you were dangerous." He clapped him on the shoulder, and then turned and went for the cracker aisle. Pete Tsiminis and Cletus Stein were behind him. Pete Tsiminis was temperamental, the fountain in his mouth. Cletus Stein was meek, as was the constancy. Jonathon had grabbed the cinnamon graham crackers. Pete Tsiminis and Jonathon and Cletus Stein went to the register. They paid for their marshmallows and their cinnamon graham crackers with the fourteen dollars, and they got about seventy-five cents in change, which went into the pocket of Jonathon, who had taken the bag of the ingredients, the large marshmallows and the cinnamon graham crackers, and went back outside into the Newfoundlander afternoon, which was cool, both Pete Tsiminis and Jonathon had agreed, with reverence and with gallantry.

The intersection of Piccadilly Street and Basalt Road was of importance. It was in that intersection the meek Cletus Stein continued onwards and the two, Pete Tsiminis and Jonathon, made the left-hand turn towards the homes. In the back of the two houses were the Betulaceæ woods, which was a constancy throughout the houses in the area of Piccadilly Street, and which was an expansive area for all people of the small and privatized community, bordered by the ambivalent houses of those who did live on Basalt Road and many other roads and also bordered by the transparent lines in between civility and unrefined Newfoundland and Labrador. Many a time, in the summer time with frequency, Pete Tsiminis and Jonathan went out into the Betulaceæ to see and examine the differences in the beaver dam, which was reconstructed every spring, and which enlarged, too, with every passing revolution; the igneous and metamorphic rocks, on either side of the beaver dam, were a well and naturalistic fundament to the seeming and nondescript constructions.

They, this afternoon, went into the Betulaceæ, not to visit the beaver, nor to see the beaver dam, but to collect sticks, or skewers for the large marshmallows they had picked up from the Coleman's. Into the Betulaceæ, Pete Tsiminis and Jonathan walked past the sack, which held the fire wood for the evening; in the hand of Pete Tsiminis was a small saw, which his father had given him minutes prior their entry into the woods and minutes following the father and son reunion, after the school day, in the kitchen, with the cabinets and the countertops, which had reformed themselves back into cabinets and countertops, from their nocturnal hammock assumptions, and Pete Tsiminis and Jonathan were in the Betulaceæ, dodging Sheep Laurel and in search for six sticks, about twenty four inches in length. The six sticks were found, in subsequence, one of about eighteen inches, another three of about twelve inches, and two of a length in between twelve and eighteen inches, the two virtuosos working in harmony to reach the sticks and saw them down to the Betulaceæ wood floor, to then rescind back into the house of the Tsiminis and collect their ingredients, the large marshmallows and cinnamon graham crackers from the Coleman's and a few bars of chocolate from the pantry, to put all of which on the countertops. The large marshmallows and cinnamon graham crackers were where Pete Tsiminis and Jonathan had left them, that is on the countertops, and in the pantry what was to be found was not a typical box of chocolate, but a box of chocolate, which held chocolate of the darkest kind, and which read on its label 90% cocoa, and made the mouth pucker. "I do enjoy dark chocolate more so than milk chocolate, Pete. I'm glad your parents got these instead of your typical schmo chocolate."

Pete Tsiminis did not mind. Jonathan always talked the way he wanted to talk. Many times it was not appropriate; but Pete Tsiminis did not mind, and he, too, did enjoy dark chocolate more so than, as Jonathan had put it, your typical schmo chocolate, but he did not mind the your typical schmo chocolate either, and did not say anything to differentiate the two, not to Jonathan, nor to his parents, and not even to himself, because it was a pleasure to be in Newfoundland and Labrador in the wintertime, and because there really was no concern, during winter and, with definitiveness, during winter in Newfoundland and Labrador, which did have a tendency to harden up and be a puncher.

1453

The homestead was the homestead of Pantagathus for a couple of nights. He got to sleep on the bed, which was in the single room house, as opposed to sleeping on the ground, where he had claimed himself a ruffian in duress. Tavis, the heretic, had gone to the homestead he had mentioned on the night of their reconnoitering. It was the house of the builder of the guitars, and Tavis, the heretic, had gone there, he said, to acquire strings for the instrument, which he had played on the night of their reconnoitering, and also had muttered inaudible excuses for escaping the small household, which was the homestead of Pantagathus for a couple of nights—"I'll have to go and—require this and that for persons prefulent for unitary operisms"—and Tavis, the heretic, was off, northwards, and Pantagathus was the maintenance person for the homestead and also for the garden, which had been developed in the past three months Pantagathus and Tavis, the heretic, had been sharing the small building in Kosmidion.

The small garden, which had a disparaged amount of herbs for seasoning and buds for steeping, had been expanded into double the size it had been, beforehand, the garden being enough to satiate one at that point, and now it was enough to satiate four or five, in the peak of the harvest season, which was the season in which Pantagathus had found himself in the hills and tending the small and tawdry parallelogram; chamomile was along the northernmost row of plants—Pantagathus had begun to take an old tendency towards the herb, one tendency, which one may call a childhood constant, and which had recurred in Pantagathus thirty years, foremost. In the evening times, when the chamomile was not being attended, and when the small building was lightened with candles made of recyclable wax, Pantagathus and Tavis, the heretic, played what Tavis, the heretic, called shim poker, a game, which he had derived from a remote priori, and which required a deck of playing cards, with three of the high cards removed, one of the Man and one of the Lady and one of the Jest, and mathematics were involved and there was color coordination and Tavis, the heretic, seemed to make up rules as they went, and the rules seemed, to Pantagathus, a little inconsistent. In a game of shim poker, ceramics had surfaced in conversation and a kiln was then desired by the two, to make plates and tiles for the floor and for the garden and, per happenstance, tiles for a small area by the creek, and tiles for the table, on which the game of shim poker was ensuing—the kiln would be small. The ceramic to make a kiln, or something to than effect, would require a bigger kiln or a forge, Pantagathus and Tavis, the heretic, able to apprehend neither of which, and the decision had been made to create small and bowed pieces, with an open fire, and then forge the pieces with adhesive of likewise material and create the small kiln, which would be about four cubic feet, all taken into consideration and in finality. The objective was to be completed, but it was not a priority, both Pantagathus and Tavis, the heretic, had agreed. In the kiln's stead, the chamomile was to be tended, as was the wheat, which was to sprout twice as full in a short while, and which was to bake bread, in the kiln, for all Tavis, the heretic, cared, once it was finished and a finished inclusion to the effects of the building; barrels of wine were around the side of the building, a grape vine to the perpendicular wall of the building, around the corner, facing the north and the chamomile, and Pantagathus was making a whistle. It was near complete, with its swipes of wooden shavings, and with the hole. For what Pantagathus wanted a whistle, he did not know. He did not even like making the whistle, but it was a pursuit, which had been challenging in the two nights Tavis, the heretic, had been northward, in the builder of the guitars homestead. He was also to create a wicker chair, for comfort, out of the fine wood, which was, too, northwards.

The chamomile had been attended. Pantagathus decided to visit the stream. He brought the stick made for fishing. The fish in the stream were small and edible. They were quite yummy, even whole and not gutted. It depended on the individual. A fish of that type and size could well be a delicate bite, and another fish of the same type and the same size could have the guts of another size, viscosity, and flavor, a quizzical exchange, which had happened three times to Pantagathus. Tavis, the heretic, had said he had not had any particular fish in his years in this building, but Pantagathus well knew he was Tavis, the heretic, and it may have been the case that he did not even know to what he was listening, in any lax normality. Pantagathus went to the stream to catch these fish, because they were yummy, and he did not deny their advantage. He did walk through the woods, northwards, and not as near as northwards as Tavis, the heretic, had walked through the woods, for guitar strings and hasheybbarder. The stream was clear and foamy.

It had been five or ten minutes of Pantagathus, with the string in the water, and with the worms on the hook, and then he caught four of the small fish, fast and in subsequence. They were collected on the ground and toiled for sixty seconds, and then they lay still. The water, which was clear and foamy, had a black and bulbous rock, nearing the bank, on which Pantagathus was fishing. The black and bulbous rock had gotten nearer, and then it had formulated a head, with eyes and nostrils, and four feet, and behind the black and bulbous rock, which Pantagathus could well see was not a rock at all, but a Batrachian of significant size, a snapper turtle, was a tail. The snapper turtle approached the bank, from which Pantagathus was watching the Batrachian, with the barrels of wine behind the homestead, in mind; and then, Pantagathus went into the stream, which had a water surface thigh deep, at its deepest depth, and retrieved the turtle, with ease, and it did not even snap. It rescinded into its shell, a complied stoic.

Pantagathus had taken off his shirt and had put the four small fish and the snapper turtle in the shirt, once back on the banks of the stream; and he headed back southwards, towards the homestead, where he would cook the snapper turtle, with immediacy. The fire of the morning's proino, of toast, was still smoldering and smoke was still visible from the fire pit. The effects for a turtle stew were on the side of the building, beside the door, that is the pot and the suspension contrivance, from which the pot would hang and cook the snapper turtle. The wine was in the back of the house, and with plentitude. Much wine was to find its way into the stew, along with beans and onions. Pantagathus prepared the pot and he gutted the snapper turtle, and then went inside of the house for the flint. Also, he picked up a handful of tinder from beside where the pot and suspension had been, and retrieved the iron fire poker, too. The fire had been ignited, the turtle meat and the beans and the onion and wine went into the pot, and Pantagathus went into the house to retrieve his whistle, which he continued to whittle, with his knife and his prod.

The turtle stew finished, Pantagathus poured himself two ladles of stew, and he began to eat the stew, with the wine and with the beans, which turned granular in his mouth, and with the onions, which were cut into quadrants. The meal was satiating. He was quite filled with the stew, and he went inside for a cut of the bread, which was in the kitchen. He cut a slice of the bread, which Tavis, the heretic, had gathered from his acquaintance, whom he was visiting these two days, northwards, and Pantagathus could not apprehend how Tavis, the heretic, arrived at the possession of the bread, nor what he did to acquire the bread; it could have been farm work or work around the household in the north or it could have been a pure and philanthropic offer to Tavis, the heretic, from the builder of the guitars, and Pantagathus decided he would not ask for the peculiarities. Instead, he went outside with his slice of bread and finished his turtle stew, with the wine soaked into the bread and cleaning the bowl, with the starchy dessert. He wanted to go to the bathroom. The stream was not far away and Pantagathus, in this time of day, about three-quarters of descension of the Helios, walked back northwards towards the stream. Once at the stream, he got naked and waded out into the stream. He alleviated himself and washed his body, and he was not using the soap he had brought from Constantinople, three months prior. He had not used the soap once. Neither had Tavis, the heretic. Pantagathus found he could well remain decent with the usage of the stream and only the stream, and he was saving the soap for a time of actual need, Pantagathus quite œconomical. He washed his butt and his armpits, and he was feeling quite well when he escaped from the stream and walked back to the homestead, with nakedness. He was to dry in the Helios, for forty-five minutes to an hour, and then he would lie in the bed until Tavis, the heretic, came home and reclaimed his quarters. Pantagathus was dry from the water of the stream, in forty-five minutes, and he had been wanton and loose in his head, thinking of the books and the libraries of Constantinople, and he was feeling the heat of the fire, which still had embers, and he was feeling the crests and troughs of the wine, which had been a part of the stew he had eaten. Tavis, the heretic, would enjoy the turtle and wine and bean and onion stew as much as Pantagathus, and he, too, was to revel in the arbitration and his euress, lying and asleep, in his bed, where Pantagathus found himself, clothed and determined in the weight of a volume of an encyclopedia, which was in the book case along the far wall.

The volume was one of four. The four volumes found in the building belonged somewhere to an encyclopedia, which was incomplete, and which may well have been disowned and even thermogenisized. Pantagathus lay in the bed and he turned and placed the volume of the encyclopedia on the nightstand, finding leverage on the tall bedposts, and then heaved himself into a sitting position. The tall bedposts went upwards about a meter at the four corners of the bed, and the bedposts kept the mattress about the same height off of the floor, that is about a meter, so as to avoid any Batrachian -slumberous exchange, but the Batrachian in its typology and genus would not be one of the specimen Testudines, that is the snapper turtle; it would be an exchange with the specimen Ophidia, that is the serpent, who many a time meandered into the folds of linens of the slumberous and made death in their skins. Pantagathus arose for his exercises.

He swung the ποδός like a pendulum, and he felt the blood collect in the ποδός until it was heavy, and then he did the same with the opposite foot. He made his arms like the thresh, and felt the blood in them, too, and he made his ankles roll clockwise, and then counter-clockwise, and then clockwise, halfway, until they were in a position, as points, Pantagathus quite supine and contracted in his abdomen, and then with his legs spread and with the action of water in a tread, quite on dry land; and Pantagathus put his feet upwards, like the parallax. The erect posture, with the hands earthbound and with the feet towards the ceiling, and also with the posterior against the single room wall, was the aim of the exercises. It was Τρίτη, that is Tuesday, and it would take until next Πέμπτη, that is Thursday, to perfect.

1923

Stefangianopoulou and Hartio arrived, after some days passed. All was in order, and Stefangianopoulou and Harito, while capable in their looks, were exasperated, one could well see, in the way their faces were sallow and in the dirt caked on their skins and clothes. They did come with rancor. They, also with their sallow exasperation, were excitable, to what end neither Panagiotis nor Santeia knew, and, in all of actuality, neither of Panagiotis nor Santeia cared about the reason why the two returned travelers were excitable—the two, Panagiotis and Santeia were in a perpetual and licentious window, which had closed, with the return of Stefangianopoulou and Harito, both of whom had returned with one bag more than with which they had left, and also they had a proposition, which would make itself prevalent, with immediacy. Stefangianopoulou said, "The travels were well, and the hospitality in Leptokaria were even better."

"I'm glad you have returned, in order," said Santeia.

"Of course, it would be no other way."

Harito opened his bag and removed a smaller bag from its contents. Stefangianopoulou and Harito were riding, one on either side of the wagon, Stefangianopoulou on the right-hand side and Harito on the left-hand side, and

Harito said, "The family in Kassitera had given us a little bit, for the return travels." Harito threw the small bag, which came from the big and additional bag, into the wagon, from his specimen Equus caballus, and Panagiotis opened the small bag and removed four boiled eggs.

"You have returned with something from your travels, Harito. Stefangianopoulou, I do hear you saying, in mind, you were not to do any such thing, as per your disagreeability."

Stefangianopoulou said, "Eat your eggs, kouto."

Panagiotis took a bite of a hard boiled egg. "You've apprehended more than your neurosis."

"That's enough, kouto."

The two, who had arrived, Stefangianopoulou and Harito, did arrive with many extra effects. They had twice as much weight to carry back to the procession as they had when they left the procession. It was not an unexpected, or spurious exchange they had had in Kassitera, nor was it an inevitability that the children of the uncle and aunt of the family of Harito and Santeia, who were the cousins, were to agree with such favorability. It all happened, and with a seeming accord—Harito had made a kill in Eptadendros. He had loaded up a family of hares with his pistol and brought the hares to the hometown of Kassitera, where they, the riders, Stefangianopoulou and Harito, and the hares, were met with conviviality. The hares of smallest size were cooked, in the evening, of which the number was five, and one adult hare was saved for the morrow's, or, per happenstance, the following morrow's evening, salted and stowed in a small barrel, to retain its freshness; and in the stead of the meat of the hares, the two riders, Stefangiano-poulou and Harito, were given a bag of dry meat, and the bag was not small to any peculiar eyes, and the bag of dry meat was also thrown into the wagon from the left-hand side and the side of Harito. "It has been granted," he said, "the invitation to reside in Kassitera, with the cousins, and with the cured meats."

Panagiotis said, "Hard boiled eggs and cured meat may not be enough to have me settle in Kassitera. In all honesty, perhaps I am go further eastward and settle in a remote place, or an even more remote place than Kassitera and Eptadendros."

"They have many heads of sheep. They have expanded. They do want help with the heads and with the farms. Don't ignore the invitation, Panagiotis, because it may be the best decision you have."

"I agree with you, in a small way."

"They have wine and it is the best wine in the town, Eptadendros even, and they sell it to the neighbors and the neighbor towns."

"That is pervasive."

"It is a well-decided route, if you were to decide to join us in our residence at Kassitera."

"I am not against it," Panagiotis said, and it was not a lie. He was not against it, and the deliberation was to last ten more minutes. The decision to move to the small town in Eptadendros was the matter, and Kassitera was to have four more residents, within ninety-six hours of the reconnoitering of the two, Panagiotis and Santeia, and the two riders, Stefangianopoulou and Harito, with adiposity.

The farm in Kassitera had been expanded. They had, as Harito said, many heads of sheep, about twenty and one hundred heads of sheep, and they had gardens, which one may well call plantations, though the gardens, or plantations were not of such a substantiality; more so, they were meant to sustain the household, of which the four—Panagiotis and Santeia, and Stefangianopoulou and Harito—were to be a part, and also to sustain the town of Kassitera and also the smaller towns, down Sappon-Kirkis, which was the road, which went through Kassitera. In the expansion of the farm, the family, who were to take in the quadric induction, and who were quite capable in horticulture, had created an herb, which was a botanic hybrid, and which was a part oregano, and a part all-spice, and a part garlic, in their small laboratory, which was in the back of the homestead, and which may well be called a standard garden. The laboratory was a ten-square foot quadrangle. It was bordered on all sides by the lumber from Eptadendros, and cut in twain. The laboratory was inside of a small area, which was fenced in by wood, which was, too, from the lumber of Eptadendros; and the children of the cousins of Santeia and Harito, that is the nephews and the nieces of Santeia and Harito, diddled in the laboratory area, with the fence and with the pejoratives—toddlers amongst the adolescents, swinging ropes and procuring sounds of sharp winds with the ropes and even sharper strophe with their manipulability.

"I still do not feel convicted on the subject," said Panagiotis.

"They do have the distillery," said Harito, and Panagiotis did smarten his nose. The distillery, the tubes and the casks, were in the shed, in Kassitera, and Panagiotis conceived evenings of discord and abandon.

"Oh, yes," said the smartened Panagiotis. "Oh, yes. The eggs and the cured meats and the wine and the heads and distillery. It does look as though, yes, Harito, it does look as though Kassitera will be the location of a rotund pascha."

"We will leave the preparations for you, this coming pascha," said Stefangianopoulou. "I do want to leave for Kassitera. First, I am going to smoke this cigaro." He removed from his front pocket a cigaro and also a matchbook, and he lit the cigaro, heading onwards, with the procession, which was to be of four individuals fewer, within twenty minutes, and Panagiotis made the note to bid regards to Tassi, the artist, who was some parties rearwards.

Panagiotis said, "Are you telling me they have tobacco on the plantations in Kassitera, too?"

Stefangianopoulou said, "They have tobacco on the plantations in Kassitera."

"What don't they have on the plantations in Kassitera?"

"Your labor."

"Not yet."

"You will be working with the heads, I presume." Stefangianopoulou was smoking his cigaro. "That's where I would put you. They have girls for the plantations."

"How many girls?"

"Many girls. They all live in the houses in Kassitera. The girls of the old man don't work on the plantations. That's what the girls of the town are for and they get received herbs and wine and this."

"The old man," said Harito. "He just sharpens his blades, just sharpens his blades, all day every day, sharpens his blades, sharpens his blades."

The cigaro in between the fingers of Stefangiano-poulou was burned down three quarters of its length. The question was what to do with the wagon and burros. They had been tied to the wagon in front of them and were walking along with the procession, with obviation. Panagiotis did suggest Tassi receive the wagon and burros in his possession. "Who is Tassi?" said Stefangianopoulou.

"He is an artist some parties behind our own, in this procession. He is a particular man, of few years, and a little aggressive," said Panagiotis. "Tassi is deprived, but he is able."

Stefangianopoulou said to Panagiotis, "Give the wagon and animals to Tassi, the artist, who is deprived, but able. I do want to leave to Kassitera."

"It will be done, in ten minutes, and then the four of us will gather our belongings and bound into Eptadendros. We have few items, only this box of a few items. We must ride slow to avoid hematoma and accidents." Panagiotis was dismounting the wagon, and heading backwards towards the party, of which Tassi was a part. The effects of the wagon, that is the wagon and the burros, would be of his effects in the finalistic exchange, following which the four—Panagiotis and Stefangianopulou, and Harito and Santeia—would divulge into Eptadendros, riding doubles.

1453

The thicket, within which was the small building, was an undiscoverable area. The foliage was well grown up on all sides of the small building, which was constructed as if in symbiosis with the vines and the thorns, in the beginning of its conception, which was well before Tavis, the heretic, had assumed its residence, Pantagathus noticed, because of its darkened walls and because of the divides in the wood, which had begun to covalence, with the aging, and harden, with the carbon dioxide. The black composite of the building was covered almost in full, by the verdant foliage and in a helter-skelter disparagement. The foliage let through a few and porous black flecks. That the building was within a seeming and undiscoverable location, from the southward, was deceptive in that the northward side of the building was a small and spacious area, of the garden, with the chamomile, and with the fire pit, and with the front door. On the three sides, which were not of the spatial side of the building, the coverage with vines and the thorns was amidst and entwined with vines of the grapes, which made the wine in the homestead, and all was meandering and bucolic. The canopy above the homestead, too, was of substantiality. It did lend total coverage. The thicket, in which the small building was located, was an exclave, and neither Pantagathus nor Tavis, the heretic, considered the decision a problem to let the fires burn out, in the evening, nor to let the fires burn well in the afternoon, when the smoke would otherwise be visible in a field or village. The relinquishment, of which Pantagathus had become a part, and of which Tavis, the heretic, had been a part for years in this building in Kosmidion, and maybe even in all his years, was the indiscriminant and loosened graciousness of both of the residents in that building, both of whom were well hermits, and together they were not separate and they were not sovereign and they were not conjoined, nor were they at hand; but they were an acquisition of that verdure, which was attrited, and which was of severity, a stark and blazing τ through the soils of Kosmidion and, too, the frontal lobes of Pantagathus and Tavis, the heretic, both of whom had been composed of collagen and bravura.

The fingers of Pantagathus had been dexterous in their whittling. The whistle was finished. It sounded like a daffy hopper. The whistle found itself in the front pocket of Pantagathus. It was wonky.

The fingers, which had created the whistle, did not find themselves in the directions of the nebulous constellates. They had not manifested warts, nor had they been abused; and Pantagathus, with the linen shirt, and with the soil, was immaculate in his gazed composure, and he was quite lacquered, in his countenance, when Tavis, the heretic, appeared and broke through the wood and into the small and spacious northward side of the building, "Good evening," the loon, and Pantagathus was glad with the return of Tavis, the heretic. He had been expecting it.

"Good evening, Tavis. How were your travels?"

"Tiresome and ingratiating."

"In all seriousness?"

"Wot and fruitful."

"I am glad."

"I am in want of a bath."

"Make the stream well."

"It was a fruitful travel, I tell you, Pantagathus. It was very fruitful and it was very wot."

"Have you come with your strings?"

"What did you just say?"

"Have you?"

"I have many strings, twelve strings."

Pantagathus said, "The guitar person is well, too, I presume?"

"He is well. He is well. He has made a drink. He has made much of one drink."

"Was it tasteful?"

"The drink he made was tasteful, and it is of importance. It is a drink of drinks, a drink of all mannish drinks, a drink of superior drinks."

"I am glad—"

"—and I am in want of a bath," said Tavis, the heretic. "I want bubbles," said Tavis, the heretic. "I want bubbles. I want bubbles," quite hysterical. "I want bubbles."

"Do you need the soap, Tavis."

"The soap, yes, I want the soap, and then we will eat a meal of—"

"—turtle stew."

"Of turtle stew. Yes, of turtle stew. I am to get the soap and to return, with cleanliness."

"It is an enjoyable evening. Have a good bath."

"I will have a good bath, Pantagathus, I can assure you."

"Wash your beard."

"I don't crane my head anymore," said Tavis, the heretic. He was inside of the homestead then, and he came outside, into the descending evening, with the soap in his hand, and he went to the stream to bathe; and Pantagathus ignited the kindle.

Eating the turtle stew, Tavis, the heretic, suggested that which was suggested to him, while visiting the homestead of the maker of the guitars, and the suggestion was one of an invitation of both Tavis, the heretic, and Pantagathus, in some weeks, when the two, who lived southwards needed to visit and make laxness, with he, the maker of the guitars, and also his girls and work hands, because there was a festive weekend imminent and the two, from the southward parts of Kosmidion, Tavis, the heretic, and Pantagathus, were, of course, invited and to bring their most burlesque persons, for the weekend of demarcation, which would not cease for seventy-two hours. "The turtle stew is well cooked," said Tavis, the heretic. "How have you made the turtle in the stew?"

"I was fishing for the fish, who have been railing me, and I saw the large amphibian come down the stream, and I snatched it from the waters. It didn't even take a snap at me, Tavis. It was well all the way into the wine—"

"—where it was even better."

"Quite right, Tavis."

"Is there anymore of the turtle meat?"

"There is more turtle meat, but not much. Have wine."

"Ladle me the turtle meat and put wine."

Pantagathus ladled in the turtle meat and put wine.

"More wine."

Pantagathus put more wine. "The maker of the guitars has girls?" said Pantagathus.

"His name is Yves Albatrois."

"Yves Albatrois has girls?"

"Yves has girls. He has four girls."

"Are they of adult age?"

"Three of the girls are of adult age, one of those three just in her twenties. He has one girl of sixteen."

"They sound a marvelous lot."

"They sound marvelous in rhythm. More wine."

Pantagathus put more wine. "Are we to go to the homestead of Yves Albatrois, in the summertime?"

"The festivities are in the latter part of summer."

"It will be hot."

"The festivities are in one week."

"In all seriousness?"

"Quite serious. The festivities are in one week. It won't be hot, with luck."

Pantagathus said, "The house must be well built to have such a festivity."

"It is well built, that house," said Tavis, the heretic. "It has three floors, smaller the higher one climbs up the stairs, and there is a basement, in which I will reside for the majority of the festivities."

"You'll reside in the basement for the festivities until Kosmidion turns into the basement, and the basement into Kosmidion." Pantagathus ladled more wine into his cup. "That may happen with more rapidity than you have foreseen."

"It would not surprise me."

"Nothing does, Tavis, the heretic. Nothing does surprise you anymore, does it?"

Tavis, the heretic, said, "I am going to have to bring wheat to the festivities. I am going to have to bring a sack. Yves needs something for compensation of the strings I brought home earlier this afternoon."

"Why not?"

"We can alternate carrying the wheat."

"Of course, and how far is the homestead of Yves Albatrois, the maker of the guitars?"

"It is to the stream, and then five or six times distant."

"That is not too strenuous."

Tavis, the heretic, said, "It will not be strenuous. More wine."

Pantagathus put wine. Pantagathus also put wine in his cup. He drank wine, every night, and not to an excess. He had begun to take, as a sleeping area, the ground outside of the building, close by the dark walls of the spacious side of the building, where it was not grown with vines and with thorns. It was either the wine, making him sleep with such affectation, or it was a heightened tolerability. Pantagathus did not care which one was the case, nor did it matter to Pantagathus, who was lying on the ground, with the empty sacks and with the linen, with the brouhaha of the cicadas and with the tolerability, or affinity; the vagrancy of the drink, which had been consumed in abundance, had incited a furiousness, which was lithe, and a stark shutter was heard and had awoken Pantagathus from his assent, and he shimmied closer the wall of the building, the spherical abdomen, the sumac weave materialized and of acme.

2017

The sticks were unrefined. They had not made them into skewers. It was around six o'clock. The Newfoundlander ambience was returned. It always did return, in the Newfoundlander coyness. It powdered the faces of the Newfoundlanders. Pete Tsiminis and Jonathon were awaiting the pallid coyness to take over, in full, and then be ambient once more, in the cut darkness of the house on Basalt Road, where the family of Jonathon osmosed into the rearward grasses of the Tsiminis household, which was, like the house of the family of Jonathon, backed by the Betulaceæ wood and further and temperate precision. They, the two young acquaintances, who lived as neighbors, collected the tinder and brought over firewood, from the sack of firewood beneath the window of the bedroom of Pete Tsiminis, and went inside of the house for two lighters.

The parents, all four of the parents, were in the kitchen, with the cabinets and with the countertops, and were discussing what sounded to Pete Tsiminis as the algæ in the harbor. He listened for only a second, and then he asked for the lighters, which were given over to him, and Pete Tsiminis and Jonathon went outside into the exact location, where the s'mores were to be smattered. The fire was started.

The tinder caught, with ease. The conic fire wood was placed, and Pete Tsiminis took his pocketknife out of his front pocket. They had gotten six sticks from the Betulaceæ, and Pete Tsiminis made of them six skewers, the tops of the sticks flaked with the feigned movements of the wrist, and then the sticks were skewers, and Jonathon went inside to retrieve the supplicants. The five came outside, and in the hand of the father of Pete Tsiminis was a case of Pabst Blue Ribbon, which would be drinked for the duration of the evening of s'mores and incisiveness. The Phil Collins record had been started, on the speakers. It was Phil Collins, and Pete Tsiminis did not go past his chrome head, in lying judgement, not in his voice nor in his lyricism. The large marshmallows were perched on the sharpened ends of the six skewers, and the browning of their persons, and then their blackening, made Phil Collins Phil Collins. The six were around the conic fire, and had made their large marsh-mallows. The cinnamon graham crackers and the chocolate, which was made with 90% cocao, and which made the mouth pucker, were segmentated into the northernized and phenomenal s'more, and by six times in that evening of senescence, with the smoke and with the smoke. The father of Pete Tsiminis had lit a smoke. He was smoking and eating a s'more. The Phil Collins turned to Peter Frampton, and Pete Tsiminis noticed the stereo was on shuffle, which was all right. The two fathers had been drinking. There was tomfoolery, and then there was raillery, which made Peter Frampton Peter Frampton. The song changed to Pearl Bailey, and Pete Tsiminis lost his inhibition. It was in the seconds' more that Pete Tsiminis glanced out into the

Betulaceæ. It was foreboding and maleficent. The Levanah, which was quite illumined, elucidated the Betulaceæ, and Pete Tsiminis noticed Jonathon was, too, looking at the sparse woods, and he knew Jonathon and he would go into the sparse woods.

Jonathon said, "It is bright."

Pete Tsiminis said, "It gets bright, in the wintertime. On good nights in gets bright."

"Look at it," said Jonathon. "You can see the craters, and it's kind of mucked. It is defined, though."

Pete Tsiminis said, "I don't look at the planets."

"It's the moon, Pete. It's not a planet."

"It's a planet."

"It's not a planet. It's the moon, Pete."

"Does it stay in the sky?"

"Yes."

"Does it have round features?"

"Yes."

"It's a planet."

"It's not a planet."

"It's a planet. It's a planet. It's a p—"

"It's the moon, Pete. It's the moon."

"It's a planet. It's a planet."

Jonathon said, "It's the moon."

"It's a planet. It's a planet."

"Tell you what we'll bet, Pete. You find me in the woods and it's a planet."

"It's a planet."

"Find me in the woods and it's a planet."

"Go into the woods."

"Pete, find me in the woods and it's a planet." Jonathon went into the Betulaceæ, with no light that was ignited. He had a flashlight, but it was not to be ignited. Jonathon was to hide in the woods, behind the houses of the Tsiminis family and the family of Jonathon, and he did not need to be found to ensure Pete Tsiminis the mucked and defined planet was a planet. Pete Tsiminis gave Jonathon three minutes in the Betulaceæ wood, and then Pete Tsiminis went out, in subsequence, with his ignited flashlight and with the mesmerized Betulaceæ.

He had been dipping in and out of small pockets of clarity, the gray epidermal of the trees raveled into one another and thin and systematic. The trees were disparaged, and in a few places in the wood, they collected with more density, and in a few places in the wood, they were sparing, in their personage. Pete Tsiminis was in the Betulaceæ, for five minutes. His light was on the gray trees, and they had begun to look inseparable from one another—they were all gray and they were all about ten inches in diameter, from one side of the tree to the other side of the tree, where Pete Tsiminis and his adolescent height found themselves, at eye level, and seeing the gray trees and the gray light, from the light in his hand and from the planet, and also the tawdry wood, beneath his feet, which were inside of boots—the direction on his left-hand side had become illumined, off twenty meters to his left-hand side, and Pete Tsiminis went towards the illumination, which was not of the light in his hand, nor the light from the planet, which was a planet, both could agree, because Jonathon had been found, and he was sitting against a tree, with his butt on the tawdry wood floor and with his back against the gray and foldable Betulaceæ. "It is a planet, Jon. It is a planet."

The light from the flashlight of Jonathon was upwards. It was making the canopy of the Betulaceæ visible. Jonathon said, "I have twisted an ankle. It hurts." He had his ankle clutched. "Help me up and take me home, back to the fire."

"Can you stand?"

"Take my hand."

Pete Tsiminis said, "Don't put weight on it." He lifted up Jonathon, and Jonathon put his arm around the shoulders of Pete Tsiminis. The lights were tripartite—the two flashlights and the planet—and Pete Tsiminis and Jonathon hobbled towards the houses and the fire, both of which were fifty meters, forwards. The fire pit was visible, too, which made the prevalent lights a quadric prevalence, and the fire pit and the fire inside of it were the only coquina luminescence of the four lights of prevalence, Pete Tsiminis, with Jonathon on his shoulders and with vigor, breaking through the wood and into the rearward grasses of the Tsiminis house, saying, "Ankle. It's an ankle." Cher was on the stereo system. There was raillery. It had become a turn towards seriousness. Jonathon sat down at the chair close the fire pit, where he had been sitting, smattering s'mores, prior the bet being placed and prior the entrance into the Betulaceæ woods.

The father of Pete Tsiminis said, "How goes it, Jonathon? What do you think about this?" The ankle had started to swell, and it was noticeable and not too bad. "Does it have much pain? How about a 1 to 10, 1 being the least painful and 10 being the most painful."

"It hurts pretty bad."

"A rolled ankle is more painful than a broken ankle."

"Do you need an ice cream?" said the father of Jonathon. "Do you need a Pabst Blue Ribbon?"

The mother of the injured said, "Be serious."

"Okay, I'll be serious." The father of Jonathon went close to Jonathon, and said, "Do you need a PBR?"

The father of Pete Tsiminis said, "We'll give him a day or two and if the swelling doesn't recede, we'll bring him to the hospital, for an X-ray."

The father of the injured handed Jonathon a Pabst Blue Ribbon, which Jonathon took into his hand. "Put it on the ankle," a suggestion, which was taken by Jonathon, the injured, and Jonathon rested his ankle on the case of Pabst Blue Ribbon, which his father hand put in front of his chair, for his injury.

The ligaments in the ankle were swollen. No ligaments had been torn and no tendons had been broken, and that was fortunate, because it was an evening of acquisition; the antibodies worked, automatic.

1923

Panagiotis had gotten off of the wagon, which was to be the wagon of Tassi, following the exchange about to occur. He walked slow, towards Constantinople. The procession moved onwards, and Panagiotis walked slow, towards Constantinople, and it was as if he were walking with rapidity.

Panagiotis reached the former wagon of Tassi as the former wagon of Tassi reached Panagiotis. Panagiotis grabbed the wagon post, with right hand, and then he swung his foot onto the step, and went into the wagon, in the same way he had when he went to inquire about the sketch of the procession Tassi had drawn. Tassi was lying down; his eyes were closed, and his hands were on his bare chest. He was a thin person; one could see the ribs and the clavicles, both of which were prominent when the artist, Tassi, was shirtless. His pants were rolled up, and his hands were still and slender and fine. "Tassi," said Panagiotis.

"Could it be Panagiotis?"

"It is Panagiotis. Kali mera, Tassi. Tell me what you think about this suggestion—"

"What suggestion?"

"I'm about to tell you my suggestion."

"Tell me the suggestion."

"—Santeia and her brother and Stefangianopoulou and I are leaving to a village called Kassitera—"

"—Kassitera, such a good name."

"—and we want you to take the wagon into your possession, and also the burros, of which there are two."

"You need to give me your wagon and burros."

"We are going to Kassitera, and want to get rid of the wagon and burros, of a good accord. We are going to Kassitera, and I would have no other person than you to reclaim the wagon and the burros."

"Go to Kassitera. I'll take care of the wagon and the burros."

"Are you sure?"

"My father will aid me with the work in transporting them to our destination," said Tassi.

Panagiotis said, "Very well. Tassi, take care of your fingers. They are a rarity. Also, there are many linens in the wagon and we cannot take all of them to Kassitera."

"I will take care of them and my fingers."

"Geiasas."

"Kalo taxithi," said Tassi, and he remained lain and was at ease.

Panagiotis grabbed the post with his left hand and swung his right foot down to the ground. He was to catch the wagon, which was the latter wagon of Tassi, and was walking with actual rapidity, the procession proceeding, with constancy.

Stefangianopoulou said, "Are we prepared?"

"The wagon," Panagiotis said, "has been granted to Tassi, the artist."

"Good," said Stefangianopoulou. "Let us load the mounts and commence with the travels." The bags, of which there were four, were loaded with foodstuffs in one bag, and in the other were the pistol of Harito and also a couple of knives and binds, which may have been in want in a circumstance, in the woods of Eptadendros. The box, within which were the silver cups and literature written by Constantinople literaries, leather gloves and a rolling pin and writing utensils, shoes and blouses and empty sacks, and stained glass, which Panagiotis had made in his childhood, and unrefined cotton and silverware and chamomile, was placed in the front of the mount of Harito, of the neck of the specimen Equus caballus. The riding arrangements were Harito and Santeia, with the box, on one mount, and Stefangianopoulou and Panagiotis, on the other mount— the wagon had been unloaded of its effects, besides the linens, which Panagiotis had told Tassi were resided in the wagon, and the burros each received a glance and an hard boiled egg—and the tessepartition commenced in their travels northward and westward, which would become travels of northward and eastward, once the familiar cues reached the eyes of Stefangianopoulou and Harito, in constituency.

The ride was a slow contiguity. The four, who were riding towards the village of Kassitera, were not in a repressed expense of time, and they were not kindred of mind. The ride to Kassitera, with the four riders, was to take triple the length of time as it did with only the two, who had originated the two-time trajectory.

It had been closer to the familiar cues, which told Harito and Stefangianopoulou to turn into the perpendicular road, which bounded towards Kassitera, when

Harito had spoken about the plans and the routes, which were to be taken Kassitera-bound. He was saying, "—and then, we will have to go off the road, because there is a traversable area of land and because we will cut our time in half. It is through the woods and it is quite pleasant. Stefangianopoulou and I slept in that wood, in our first travel to Kassitera. There were no hardships—"

"You're telling me we will have to sleep in the woods, with the bears and with the dogs?"

"It's not bad. It won't be bad, Santeia. It is only for one night."

Stefangianopoulou said, "It is bad and there are many animals around, in Eptadendros."

"Shh, don't say that to her," Harito said.

"It is best to be honest," said the other of the reign holders.

"Not all the time," said Harito.

"There are always the variations."

"We will find our old camp and there will be no differences outside of the number of riders we have with us."

"We will not find our old camp," said Stefangianopoulou.

"I will make you a bet we find our camp."

"What happens if I win?"

"You get stamps."

"What happens if I lose the bet?"

"I get money."

"What happens if the bears win the bet?" said Santeia.

"The bears get my money."

"It is a bet, Harito," said Stefangianopoulou. "It is a bet only because I need my Ottoman kuruş to be of value."

It had been in the intersection, with the familiar cues, which told Harito and Stefangianopoulou to turn towards the north and east, that Harito had suggested they dismount and relax for fifteen minutes, because they were well past the procession. The four did dismount from their specimens Equus caballus, and they had break. Harito and Santeia, and Stefangianopoulou and Panagiotis each ate a bit of the dry meat. Stefangianopoulou finished the remainder of his tobacco.

The creek, off of which the prior camp of Harito and Stefangianopoulou, was in the mind of Harito. He could see the familiar rocks. The creek was definitive. There was a slight bulge, in the creek, one third of the way through Eptadendros, and then the creek hung a sharp westward turn and terminated, with immediacy. In the cleft was where the former camp of Harito and Stefangianopoulou was located, and Harito had made the recognition of its nestled location. They had walked the horses through the creek, and the termination of the creek was off to the west a ways, and Harito knew it was so, because he had gone for a walk the evening prior their last day, towards Kassitera. The four individuals were riding, and had been riding for hours, towards the cues, which would initiate the entrance into the Eptadendros wilderness, which was not so arbitrary, and which was rather wistful in its verdure and in its spaciousness; the verdant grounds of Eptadendros heightened in chromatics and into viridian volumes, the further towards the canopy it incited. The peculiar rocks of the creek were not the most immediate item. In their stead, the shattered fence of some kilometers upwards took the mind of Harito, who was apprehensive in making the entrance into the grasses, and who was in the middle of a consideration to cut his hair, upon the arrival at Kassitera.

His hair had gotten longer. It was never short. The young Harito had had long hair, and the long hair had made itself a constancy, much as the tendency towards equestrianism and towards sewing. Harito had been the receptor of many criticisms, in that sewing was for girls and that sewing was for old girls, who had not an objective in their lifespans, let alone an objective of mannishness; Harito did not listen, and he was not sewing dresses, nor was he sewing pants. The articles, which came from the hand of Harito, were of equestrian kindness, and they were leather gloves and leather jackets and hats. The articles were made well and with consciensciousness. Many affiliates of Harito had received gloves and hats and a couple affiliates even received a jacket each, all articles made of leather, which was apprehended from a tanner closer Petra District, in Constantinople. The leather gloves found their way onto his hands in the most strenuous of equestrian activities, and the leather gloves were protection for their makers, and the hands were inside the leather gloves, a relationship, which was appropriate, and which had lessened in apparentness, over the recent few months. The hands of Harito were not covered by the leather gloves as the shattered fence came into sight—a sight which had surfaced along with the notion to experiment with scissors and hair stylishness upon reaching the village of Kassitera. Santeia blew into her handkerchief.

"This is the place where we go into the Eptadendros woods," said Harito.

"This is the fence I was telling you about," said Stefangianopoulou to Panagiotis.

Eptadendros, in its wilderness, was in further company. The tawdry road ceased. Eptadendros was a supple verge. It made the sullen feet of the Equus caballus appreciable; there was an immobility in the woods. It was broken by the whim of the vas. Eptadendros was of liveliness, by the kinematics of the traveler party, which was skistos in its initiative. The aquarelle assumed its capricious absolutability—the ovum was of dolefulness—and Santeia drank from a bottle of water, and, regarding the creek, her brother had contrived accuracy.

1453

The lacklustre was in perpetuity. The building was kept. The vines were growing, and they were budding grapes. The garden was also in a fructuous constant. The chamomile had been harvested. The residents drank wine and chamomile in the mornings and afternoons. In the evenings, they went back to wine. The wheat, too, was teeming with precociousness. It was all reverie. It was all euphoria. It had been high noon, and Pantagathus was having chamomile. It was yummy and made polity.

Tavis, the heretic, joined him. He took the buds from the bag and added hot water from the fire pit. The water had been set to boil ten minutes prior, and had cooled off, imbibed with the chamomile. The buds were still in the water. Neither Tavis, the heretic, nor Pantagathus minded. They chewed on the buds. The smoke was blown to the canopy, which was omnipresent. It was not an issue. Neither Tavis, the heretic, nor Pantagathus considered it a problem, and they were correct in that consideration; it had been three months in the hills of Kosmidion for Pantagathus, and no troublesome exchanges had become manifest. The two, Pantagathus and Tavis, the heretic, were drinking chamomile and three riders came from the bush, from the westward direction. They were Ottoman and were domineering. They had sabres and they were dressed in leather and metal. One of them had a distinguishable headpiece, which made him important. Neither Tavis, the heretic, nor Pantagathus made movements, and neither of them were erratic. They were drinking chamomile, and there was no problem with such an action, even if it were in the hills, undetectable, and twenty or thirty kilometers north and west of Constantinople, which had been taken ninety days prior—the nearness of the woods and foliage and the location of the building, which was situated in a small impression in the hill, was camouflage enough—protected for three months, until the riders entered in on the tea of Pantagathus and Tavis, the heretic. Pantagathus smelled chamomile from the bag, with a small touch of verity, and he envisaged the clearing southwards.

"We have no orders," said the rider with the headpiece, in Greek.

Tavis, the heretic, stood. "Welcome to the homestead of Tavis, the heretic, and Pantagathus, the doofy." He bowed, with his hands extended on either side of his body.

"We need water."

Pantagathus had arisen and went into the building. He went into the building for two reasons. One reason was for the water, for the riders. The second reason was because of what was around his neck. It had been on the first morning in the building when Pantagathus had taken off his stavrouli. The golden stavrouli had been given to him, at his baptism. He had not worn the stavrouli for the days he had been in the building, with Tavis, the heretic. The morning of the entrance of the Ottomans, he had put on the stavrouli, with assiduousness. He took off the stavrouli and put it in his pocket, and then walked outside to the Ottomans and Tavis, the heretic, with the water, which was in a large glass jug. He handed the water to the important Ottoman, who was on a gray Arabian.

The Ottoman said, "Thank you."

"It is not a problem," said Tavis, the heretic. "This is an open building and all we have is all you have."

The Ottoman dismounted his Arabian. The two other riders did also dismount. "The water is appreciated."

"As is the camaraderie," said Tavis, the heretic. "We have not seen people in months. How is Constantinople? Is there a Constantinople?"

"Constantinople is still southward. The hacking city has been destroyed. The blood still clings to the walls. Nobody needed this invasion to be of such terror."

"It is the way of Constantinople."

"What is your religion?"

"Mohammedan, of course."

"Of course."

"Have you come for conversions?"

"Have you weapons?"

"We are a tribulation voided people. Go inside and get the turtle stew, Pantagathus."

Pantagathus went inside and got the turtle stew, and, beforehand, he put the stavrouli in the drawer in the kitchen. "It is turtle stew," said Pantagathus. "I caught the turtle myself."

"Very well. Put the turtle stew on the fire. We will eat." The Ottoman took off his headpiece. "Do you have anything you need to give us?"

"We are giving you the turtle dinner." Tavis, the heretic, returned to his seat, and so did Pantagathus. The turtle stew was heated. The Ottomans sat down to the turtle stew.

There was a disagreeability to the Ottoman at hand. He was talking to people of the Byzantine empire, and he knew he was talking to a Byzantine people, and he was asinine. Pantagathus ladled three bowls of stew for the three Ottoman riders. The stew was near its end. The Ottoman rider took the spoon from the hand of Pantagathus. He stirred the stew and found a few pieces of turtle meat in the stew, and then he put the stew to his lips. He wrapped his lips around the spoon, and then he spat the stew into the fire pit. "Is there wine in this stew?"

"The stew is wine. Also, there is turtle meat." Tavis, the heretic, laughed. Pantagathus heaved laughter and attempted to make it as if he were clearing his throat. "The beans and onions are from our garden, over here. You are welcome to take a look at the plants."

"It is wine. It is not stew. It is wine. You call it stew because there are a few slices of turtle meat?"

"It is politics, general commander. It is not more than œconomics—"

"Bring bread."

"We have none. I am honest." Tavis, the heretic, had intended the bread inside to last until the festivities, the coming weekend. "There is none else here, commander. I am honest, in entirety."

"I do not like this place. Take the stew. It is yours, and it is made of wine. It is not even tasteful."

"Do whattyoo do is the hririhuroo—"

"What?"

"What?"

"You are all madmen in Byzantion," the important Ottoman said, and it was true. It was true the Byzantine people were aberrational, and the Ottoman commander knew of the aberration, which gave all in the exchange a certain and surreptitious acropachy; none were enjoying the camaraderie. "It is time we leave."

"Leave if you will," said Tavis, the heretic.

"It is two hours until barracks, and then the three of us will get sleep."

"Sleep, commander. Sleep."

"The thing is, madman, I would rather sleep around a spearhead than a schedule."

"It seems you have more so a chance making that happen if you were to climb in ranks than maintain your position. That, too, is the way of Constantinople."

"The general smokes and fucks. I do not admire him."

"None of whom are in likeness," said Tavis, the heretic. "Stay in your present position."

"Same to you."

"Stonhades."

The Ottoman mounted his Arabian. The two other riders, too, mounted their Arabians. The three riders were off, back into the bush. The tea of Tavis, the heretic, and Pantagathus had been compromised. The chamomile had gotten cold. Tavis, the heretic, poured his cup of chamomile into the soil. "Let's try that again, shall we?" Tavis, the heretic, said, and he put on the pot, with the water and with the tepidity, and Pantagathus wetted the ground with his chamomile.

1923

The four riders had been riding for six hours. It was getting towards the evening time. The ambience of the Eptadendros woods was retained. It would maintain its copiousness, for two more hours; and then, the chroma would descend, and it would be nighttime. The two, who had placed the bet, which pertained to their former camp, were in search of the cues of the creek, which, too, maintained itself, some odd meters to the east. They were northbound, and they were having exchanges with the first licks of fatigue, as were the specimens Equus caballus, who were to drink their water from the creek, once the former camp was found and Harito collected his kuruş, or once the chroma of the evening did descend and Stefangianopoulou collected his stamps. The ride had been six hours northwards, and the former camp was in close proximity, both of the gamblers knew. Neither, in all of actuality, cared about the bet; it was more so an alleviation of boredom, or stasis, which kept them in good continuation. It had been kilometers rearwards and two hours rearwards when Harito had said, "We are three-quarters of our way to the old camp." Nobody had said anything, in response. For minutes the Eptadendros trees sustained, in their wet contact.

Stefangianopoulou said, "We may well be three-quarters of our way closer to kotopoulo, rather than the old camp."

Santeia said, "Don't say that. You'll make me hungry."

"We are three-quarters of our way to the old camp," said Harito.

Stefangianopoulou said, "We may well have passed the old camp."

"Not a chance. It is ahead one hour." Two hours had passed and they had not found their former camp. The creek maintained itself, in the eastward direction. The cues had not been spotted. The peculiar rocks of the creek were not discovered. Harito said, "Let us take our mounts closer the creek, and perhaps find the cues or set camp for the evening."

Stefangianopoulou pulled his reins eastwards, without a spoken word. Harito did the same, and the creek was much closer than it had been, and the water was definitive. The water was in movement, with exactitude. The riders did think what it would be to know the smell of the creek their whole lives. Constantinople had been where they had lived.

There were no creeks inside the walls. There were no actual reasons to leave the walls. Besides the desire to venture out and into the woods, by some juvenility, it was unnecessary, and none of the four had pursued the route of seemless exploration. It had been the city was to be evacuated, and the likenesses of the four had become more so of those of expansionary people, and it was not of the accord of the riders, who were in the woods of Eptadendros, and who were in search for the former camp of Stefangianopoulou and Harito, to lie down on the verdant floors and sleep, and wake in the early morning, when the Helios had not arisen, and when the travels further north were in demand—the creek was meters to the right-hand side of the riders, and Stefangianopoulou said, "We will find ourselves in Kassitera before we find ourselves in our old camp."

"It is not so," said Harito.

"I will bet you double we find ourselves in town before we find ourselves in our old camp.

"You don't have that kind of money."

"I don't have that kind of money."

"What are you betting double, or suggesting we bet double when you don't have that kind of money?"

Stefangianopoulou said, "I don't have that kind of money, but I have an idea. The idea is for an invention. It is an idea for an invention, and if we find our old camp you will have the rights to the invention."

"What is the invention?"

Stefangianopoulou said, "Let us find the camp and then I will relay the invention to you."

"What kind of invention is it? Can I think of a better invention?"

"No, you cannot."

"If I can think of a better invention, I would not take the bet."

"I bet you you cannot think of a better invention, after you hear my invention."

"What do I get if I win the invention bet?"

"You get the invention and its labor in creating it."

"Very good."

"—and what do I get if I win?" said Stefangiano-poulou.

"Santeia."

The saliva of Panagiotis went into his mouth.

Stefangianopoulou said, "It is a bet."

"We will need the old man as a witness to the legalities, my champion," said Harito, and they rode further down the creek, northwards, in perpetuity. The had ridden for fifteen minutes longer, and the woods of Eptadendros had begun to descend in chroma. The V-shaped rock was ahead. The water of the creek tumbled through the V-shaped rock. "The rock," said Harito. "It is the rock for which we had been searching. It is the rock for which we have been searching, and the old camp is one hundred paces westwards. It is a good invention, is it not, Stefangiano-poulou?"

"It is a good invention. Let us travel westwards, one hundred paces, and we will see if the rock is the rock you had intended to find."

"It is the rock I intended to find, Stefangianopoulou," Harito said. They were riding eastwards, and the ashen ellipse came into view. It had been where Harito and Stefangianopoulou had cooked one of the small hares, days prior the rediscovery of the camp. "It is the camp, Stefan-gianopoulou. It is the camp, and here we can camp."

"Very well, navigator. It seems we have found the old camp." Stefangianopoulou was not upset. He was quite elated in that he did not expect such a punctual arrival at the old camp, and he dismounted, and then Panagiotis dismounted the same specimen Equus caballus; and Harito and Santeia, too, dismounted their specimen Equus caballus, and Harito patted Stefangianopoulou on the shoulder. Stefangianopoulou was impassive, and he said, "It looks as though it has been untouched."

Harito said, "Indeed, it does seem untouched. It has only been four days."

Panagiotis went closer the ash of the fire pit of the former camp. The bones of the small hare were in the fire pit. It read beneath the disemboweled skeleton κόκκαλο, which meant bone, and there was an arrow drawn towards the disemboweled skeleton, and there was a circle around the disemboweled skeleton.

Harito came over to Panagiotis. "I made that," he said.

"O your high mind," said Panagiotis.

Stefangianopoulou and Santeia, too, came over to the ashen fire pit and the disemboweled skeleton, with the arrow and with the circle. "He is an original."

"I'm made of bones," said Harito.

"I'm made of money," said Stefangianopoulou, who took out and handed over to Harito a sack of Ottoman kuruş, which were worthless.

2017

Pete Tsiminis and Jonathon were side by side, in the waiting room of the hospital. Jonathon had missed two days of school. It had not been so bad for Pete Tsiminis and he was concerned for Jonathon, in that the middle school and the walk home, towards the fork in the road, past the hill, with the divot and with the ditch at its bottom, and past the Coleman's, where Pete Tsiminis and Jonathon had gotten large marshmallows and cinnamon graham crackers, and Piccadilly Street and Basalt Road, where they lived, were all humorless, and they were not as titivating, in the absence of Jonathon; Pete Tsiminis arrived home, on Basalt Road, and had gone into the house of Jonathon, following a quick hello to his parents and putting down his backpack. Jonathon was in a chair, in the living room. His ankle was bound with gauze, and it was swollen and in pain, said Jonathon, and he said he and his father were going to the hospital to X-ray the ankle, because it was broken, in all probability.

Pete Tsiminis had gotten Jonathon a paper cup full of water. Jonathon drinked down the paper cup full of water, and Pete Tsiminis took the empty and conic cup and put it in the garbage can. A nurse, who was rather large, called the name of Jonathon, and the three, Pete Tsiminis, Jonathon, and the father of Jonathon, were taken into an infirmary, where people lay strew about and were ridden and injured. The nurse said to have patience. The doctor would be in, and then they would take Jonathon to get an X-ray and that it would all be over in one to two hours. Pete Tsiminis was allowed into the X-ray room. He watched Jonathon get covered in the metalloid sheet, which protected the vital organs from the X-rays, which were supposed to be dangerous; and then, Jonathon was left in the X-ray room, while Pete Tsiminis was taken into the room with the buttons and screens, which showed the ankle bones of Jonathon, and they were broken, said the X-ray technician, and he showed Pete Tsiminis the fracture.

"He will be in a cast for some weeks," said the X-ray technician. "Don't go too hard on him and don't force him to come outside and throw the ball around. He needs rest. Help him out, if he wants."

"Yes, Mister X-ray man," said Pete Tsiminis, and the X-ray technician smiled, with tight lips, and the X-ray technician and Pete Tsiminis went back in to the X-ray room to join Jonathon, who was lying beneath the sheet, and who was uncomfortable, one could well see; his face was in a grimace and his eyes were shut. He looked quite disagreeable.

"Jonathon, your ankle is broken. No doing what Pete wants. Stick to the home front. Eat and sleep well, because it does wonders for the psycho-somatics."

"How long will it be broken?"

"Six weeks rest and you will be able to do all you were able to do before the fracture."

"Thanks."

"Don't thank me. It's not good news. You're going to need a cast for six weeks. Pete can sign it for you and you will be a slow mover."

Jonathon said, "Did the X-rays affect me? Am I going to mutate?"

"You already have. In three days your skin will become transparent. Your vital organs will assume transparency, in subsequence. You will be invisible, in two weeks, like the H.G. Wells novel."

"Very good, Mister Diggs."

"Who is Mister Diggs?" asked the X-ray technician.

"You're Mister Diggs, and I am Gammaretron, the smallest and most apt to smother your mother."

"Enough, Jonathon. Let's get you to your daddy and out of this hospital."

"Very well," said Jonathon.

The X-ray technician handed Jonathon off to the nurse outside the door. "Bye, Jonathon."

"Bye, Mister Diggs," said Jonathon, and he was reconnoitered with his father, and Pete Tsiminis was saying the fracture was to be healed in six weeks—the father of Jonathon, Jonathon, the injured, and Pete Tsiminis, then went into the evening and the Newfoundlander briskness, and then into the small two door automobile, which took them northwards, towards Basalt Road.

The shops the automobile had passed, on the way towards Basalt road, were manifold. There were electronic stores and pet stores and grocery stores, and there were video stores and nutrition stores and hardware stores; and there were advertisements in some of the windows of the stores, a microwave in the electronics store window, for $15; the chicken was buy one get one at the grocery store, which the automobile had passed; the hardware store was selling a new line of power tools, and if you got three tools you got the drill with the peculiar bits, all of this unnoticed by Pete Tsiminis, and Jonathon and the father of Jonathon, too, except for the microwave oven, which was being sold for $15, because there were neon lights and because it had been in an ill lit stretch of road—the settled climate and the sallow and vibratory optics of the road, on which was the neon and the microwave oven advertisement, which sold the microwave oven for $15, was a bounding and recoiling height, which was imperceptible in all ways but one way. The cooperation was extreme. The err in the carbonate had flattened. The addendum had been low. Jonathon was to get his cast, and it was to be signed. The prior two days had allotted much time and hysterics to the travels, homewards, from the hospital. It was the comprehensive exchanges of the few days, which had proceeded the travels homewards, from the hospital, made the travels the travels. The prior two days, of the bedridden Jonathon and the humorless walks of Pete Tsiminis, with the lack of titivation and with the stasis, were of amplitudes and frequencies, which were not able for detection by the X-ray machines, and which were not received in the print outs of the electro-encephalogram, four rooms over from the X-ray rooms, the patient of which in the sights of the haphazard, and in the close distance of illusory lights and cues, which rendered one apt for inconstancy and for inconsistency, in lenses of the eyes, which went into the myelin sheaths of the stamen of the optics, which were fed into the synaptic clefts of the receptors, and their parallelisms and their prismatics—the electronic stores, with microwave for $15; the buy one get one privileges; the power tools and the bits, which were of apprehension, with common fate—and with the lethargic eyes of Pete Tsiminis and the hard cast of Jonathon and even the telegraphed words and symbols, which reached the dawdled heads of the passengers of the automobile, the err was retained, in the driveway of the house, in which the family of Jonathon lived; beside which the family of Pete Tsiminis lived.

Jonathon and his father went into their house. Jonathon was on crutches, and it would stay that way for six weeks, or until he lost patience with the crutches and decided to waddle around on his feet. Pete Tsiminis went towards his house. He meandered through a couple of the Ligustrum. Inside, his mother was in the kitchen. She was having a cup of tea, and the father of Pete Tsiminis was outside, having a smoke. It was eight o'clock P.M. Pete Tsiminis went outside, for only a second, to say hello to his father, and he went back inside, to where his mother was drinking tea. She said hi, and how was the hospital?

"It was a hospital. It was hectic," was the response from Pete Tsiminis.

"This tea is good. It is a tea I got from the apothecary, while you were at the hospital. I need you to bring a bag of this tea to Jonathon's mother. Will you do that for me?"

Pete Tsiminis said, "Sure. One second." He went to the W.C. "Where is the bag of tea?" he said, once back in the kitchen.

"Let me bag it up really fast. I haven't even bagged it up yet." The mother of Pete Tsiminis got up from the kitchen table and went to the pantry and got out a Ziploc bag, into which she put a few tablespoons of tea. "Here you go. Take that over to Jonathon's and tell his mom the tea is from the Yukon Territory. It's hydroponic."

"I'll be right back," said Pete Tsiminis, and he went outside and back through the two Ligustrum. He knocked on the door and the father of Jonathon answered the door. He stepped aside and let Pete Tsiminis inside the house, which was decorative in its Oriental rugs, and which was an open house, in its ceilings.

"Come in from the cold," said the father of Jonathon, when he had opened the door, and Pete Tsiminis did walk inside and showed the bag of tea to the father of Jonathon.

Pete Tsiminis said, "My mother needed me to come over here and bring this bag of tea for Jonathon's mom. It's from the Yukon Territory. It's hydroponic."

The father of Jonathon said, "Hold on. Let me get her." He went into the bedroom, which was further into the house, in its entry, and to the left-hand side of the living room, which was enumerated with tapestries, and which was a verdant portcullis.

The mother of Jonathon came outside of her bedroom. She said, "Pete, what could you be doing here? Your mother has sent you for something, Ty said."

Pete Tsiminis said, "My mother needed me to come over here and give you this bag of tea. It's from the Yukon Territory. It's hydroponic."

"Very considerate of her. She knows I've been looking for a new tea. I've been drinking the tea I have for so long. I have been in need of a new tea."

"Have a good night," said Pete Tsiminis.

"Good night, Pete," said the mother of Jonathon. She had gone into the kitchen, to boil water for the tea, which might have been her new tea.

"Good night, Pete," said the father of Jonathon, and he opened the door for Pete Tsiminis, who went outside into the Newfoundlander cold, and who went back through the two Ligustrum, towards his house, where he would go outside and sit with his father, if his father was still having his smoke.

He was still having his smoke, and the father of Pete Tsiminis had started a small fire in the small fire pit, which was on the elevated patio, and which was its own contained fire place. The fire place was rectangular, and at the top of the fireplace was a hearth, and the detritus fell into the bottom of the fireplace, where it could be cleaned, with a second and removable hearth. The father of Pete Tsiminis was smoking and Pete Tsiminis was munching on cinnamon graham crackers. Jonathon had left half of the cinnamon graham crackers for the Tsiminis household, and Pete Tsiminis had given half of the large marshmallows to Jonathon, for future and sovereign s'more smatter. The incisiveness was at the skin of Pete Tsiminis. The enveloped few days, in the absence of Jonathon, and in the small exchanges with the points along the road towards the fork and towards Piccadilly Street and Basalt Road, all had been flattened, expanded, and rounded, as a bake. The brown slopes of the hill had been dried, in the recent few weeks. They had assumed their wintertime person. One looked into the wood and saw the incendiary. They saw the yore. The botanics of the irascible τ had been cropped into the colline-ar π of rapid starts and retrograde ends. The snow was about to magnetize.

2017

They had made a sled, years ago. Pete Tsiminis and his father were deliberating going to the Coleman's to buy a sled, the one like a contact lens; and they found themselves at the hardware store, buying two by fours and pieces of metal, which would otherwise go onto a fire place hearth. The retailer was coerced, by the father of Pete Tsiminis. The fire place hearth would have otherwise been sold as one unit, all the parts accounted for. The father of Pete Tsiminis coerced the retailer to go ahead and break the box and give over the support structure for the fire place hearth, which would be the runners for the sled, and not without a forty-dollar bargain, which went straight into the pocket of the retailer, who was jovial, because it was the season for such conviviality. The sled had been constructed. It resided in the corner of the Tsiminis garage, for the snow seasons. It was the snow season. The sled made of two by fours and the fire place hearth runners was removed from its corner, and it was dusted off with a gloved hand of the father of Pete Tsiminis, because the hill just westwards was to be covered with powder, in two days time, said the meteorologist on the flickering contrivance, otherwise known as the television, and otherwise obsolete in the snow season. Jonathon was in his house, and he was, too, deliberating a small pursuit, which his parents were not going to condone, and which his parents were not going to discover—the weekend and the snowfall was going to find itself in the accompaniment of one more sled rider, on the hill, westwards, and it was to be Jonathon, the injured, and Pete Tsiminis was in favor of the decision of sledding with Jonathon, who was to make the decision, in agreeability.

The evening had not descended. The Newfoundlander afternoon had an hour, at its disposal, and then, it was to thicken and recompense into night. The fireplace was to be lit, on this night, too. It was not the fireplace, in the center of the Tsiminis backyard to be lit. The fireplace was to lit on the elevated patio, with the two hearths.

Hotdogs were for dinner, and the parents of Jonathon came over to the Tsiminis house, and they made hotdogs on the fire, on the patio, and it was in the crispy buns where they found most enjoyment. The Betulaceæ was further outwards. The fire, or illumination, of the fire did not reach the Betulaceæ. It was quiet, as the mothers drinked their tea.

Monday was take your baby to work day. It was not hard to convince his father to let him stay home and not go to the lab, where he worked. Instead, Pete Tsiminis was to stay home and go and see Jonathon, to keep him company and to make the first inscription on the hard cast, which was to be the name of Pete Tsiminis, and which was not the name of Pete Tsiminis, once the renascent pair got together; instead, on the hard cast two games of tic-tac-toe were played and the game of dots was drawn, following which they ate.

1923

Kassitera was on the agenda. It would be the place where the four found themselves, within six hours. It was not even a question to Santeia, who woke with the earliness of Eptadendros. She was glad to be awake. She was glad to be awake alive. Also, she was excitable, in seeing her uncles and aunts, and also the old man, who was her great uncle. The nieces and nephews were going to be fun. The country of Eptadendros had arisen into perceptibility. The indium came out of the trees, in between which was the naturalistic Eptadendros and shadows, which would alleviate themselves, in forty-five minutes. She lay in her linen for a bit longer; she went to the side to urinate and she went to the creek to drink water. Arrived back at camp, Panagiotis was eating dry meat. Santeia joined him, and they ate a couple of pieces of dry meat, and then Stefangianopoulou shouted into wakefulness, and the Eptadendros spellbindedness was finished. Harito arose. Everybody had dry meat, which was yummy, and which was depleted, almost in entirety.

It was no bother. They had bread and also they had a wedge of cheese, which they would eat on the way to Kassitera, and which would, too, be depleted upon their arrival in Kassitera. There was no question. The four would be hungry by the time of their arrival, which was to be around noon, and which was to be met with bread and wine. The plantation in Kassitera was in no scarcity, and everybody who had awoken in Eptadendros knew the plantation was at high efficiency. All four of the riders knew it was at capacity, in terms of exports, and the imports were riding Kassitera-bound within the hour, and full of stomach, in relativity.

The mounts were once again mounted in the same arrangements as they had been mounted, leaving the procession, that is, Harito and Santeia on one mount, and Stefangianopoulou and Panagiotis on the other mount, and the box, with the silver cups and the literature written by Constantinople literaries, the leather gloves and the rolling pin and writing utensils, the shoes and the blouses and the empty sacks, and also the stained glass, which Panagiotis had made in his childhood, the unrefined cotton, silverware, and chamomile, were on the mount of Stefangianopoulou and Panagiotis; they had arranged the transference to the other mount the night prior, for the sake of justice, or what remaining justice was left. The two mounts and the riders walked through the creek, with the fluidic sonics and with the chortles, from the specimens Equus caballus; they, too, were well rested and had finished the remainder of the dry meat. They had drinked from the creek, and then had gone through the white edges of the miniature currents. The riders were silent for an hour or so, and they were listening to the Ornethura creak their way into existence in that wood. It was a maintained microphony.

The wood of the Eptadendros plantæ, the Quercus and the Streptophyta, retained the oscillations and released them, back into the grove. The vibrations of a high body became audible. They were raised in decibels, and sustained a recognition from the four riders—an aircraft, overhead, was heading in the eastern and southern direction. The aircraft was visible to the four, all of whom craned their heads.

Stefangianopoulou said, "That is a Greek aircraft, if I do see well."

"Why not? Where could it be going?"

"It has got to be headed towards Smyrna. It might even get there without any damage."

"Why would an aircraft be headed towards Smyera?" Santeia said.

"For any reason. It could be for a peculiar objective. It could be for fun. It could be for any reason."

"An aircraft would be frightening."

Stefangianopoulou said, "They are even more frightening when they are shooting at you."

"Have you even been fired at by an aircraft?"

"Not once."

Santeia said, "Take us to Sappon-Kirkis." Sappon-Kirkis was the road to find. Sappon-Kirkis was the road, which was to take the four to another, convening road, which went into the homestead in Kassitera. Sappon-Kirkis was a three-hour ride, and then the village of Kassitera would find itself in the midst of four citizens anew. The escape of the Eptadendros wood, which was bordered upon Sappon-Kirkis, and which would take place in one hour, and also the road Sappon-Kirkis, was the matter; and for thirty minutes Eptadendros had never been monastery.

The dirt road staggered its way towards Kassitera. The riders were finished with their bread and cheese. The road had been en route towards Kassitera for over a hundred years. It preceded Man, who had built the road, or rather who had lain the road with their feet and with their intentions. Their feet bounded them forwards, and their feet bounded them towards their intentions, which were relevant and of their own accord; the reason of Man, in the stretches of conception, which placed the road, Sappon-Kirkis, had succeeded the four riders, who, too, did further make the road trodden and laconic. The convened road, which headed northwards, in relation to Sappon-Kirkis, made itself evident. It was so, in the white corner of the house, which was, too, a cue in navigation. The northbound road went to the northernmost part of Kassitera. Halfway through the town, the homestead of the great uncle of Santeia and Harito was located, in a raised part of land, and the mounts pulled up the inclination, in exasperated gait. Their ears turned. It was the intuition of the specimens Equus caballus told them they were close to water. It was not a body of water, which made them innocuous, nor was it the coy reception of the four riders by their cousins and nieces and nephews. It was the placated slovenliness, which made them lax. The road, Sappon-Kirkis, and Eptadendros had followed the riders into the Kassitera homestead. The procession solvated, in mind. It came from the mouths of those riders, who relayed the peculiarities of the process, and whose mouths were full, in between words regarding such peculiarities, of bread and wine; and there were kisses and there were patted face cheeks. The old man had been in from the shed. It was noon. He had known the four were to arrive today, and he was in maintenance of the distillery, which he knew was essential to the citizens anew, and which was in order, he did relay; he needed to make an entrance, with gusto. The wine and bread were eaten, and there was not much more given the four riders, who had completed their travels through Eptadendros, from the procession, because there was kotopoulo in the oven, and it was to be of much flavor. The old man took the riders, each of the four riders, to their bedrooms. Santeia had her bedroom, and Stefangianopoulou and Panagiotis their own, and Harito had a bedroom, which was, in all of actuality, a storage room—he had taken the storage bedroom of his own accord, and it was not indecent by four o'clock P.M.—the room of Santeia on the first floor, beside the storage bedroom, and the bedroom of Stefangianopoulou and Panagiotis, on the second floor, which was a loft, in all of actuality, and which was accessible by the usage of a staircase, and it was more so a stepladder than a staircase. The staircase, or stepladder, was under a dozen steps in height. The box, with the silver cups and the literature written by Constantinople literaries, the leather gloves and the rolling pin and writing utensils, the shoes and the blouses and the empty sacks, and also the stained glass, which Panagiotis had made in his childhood, the unrefined cotton, silverware, and chamomile, was unloaded. The chamomile went downstairs to the kitchen, which was beginning to thrum, with the preparation of the meal and with the girls. Also, the leather gloves were brought into the storage bedroom of Harito, who had created the leather gloves. Rolling pin and silver cups were taken to the kitchen and the room of Santeia. The writing utensils stayed in the loft, because Panagiotis was feeling a letter of emotionality was to be written on paper, which may not have found its way to his mother, who was in the procession, and who was displaced. The stained-glass Panagiotis had made in his childhood was displayed in the window, with the windowsill and with the finite amounts of smidgen. The shoes and blouses and empty sacks were strewn, systematic, on the far wall, to the left-hand and northmost side of the loft, which, too, was decent and by four o'clock, before which the patio of the homestead in Kassitera was prepared with table and with plates. The patio was located in a small corner courtyard.

1453

The guitar of Tavis, the heretic, was repaired. It had six strings. The B string had broken, which was the reason Tavis, the heretic, went to the homestead of Yves Albatrois, maker of guitars, and he had gotten the invitation to the festivities, which were to begin in seventy-two hours. Tavis, the heretic, was plucking a few strings. It was a randomized pluck of the fingers. There was no rhythm. He had been listening to the oscillations, which occurred in the in between notes, and which many times broke strings. It wobbled and Tavis, the heretic, brought it back to tune, with gaiety and with Pantagathus lying in the place, beside the building, where he slept, and Pantagathus was on his linens. The linens had been from the drawer in the kitchen of the building. They had not been used in some years, by the smell of them, when Pantagathus had taken them from the drawer, and he had washed them in the stream in the first few days of his residence in the resplendent exclave, an action, which would take place once more in sixty minutes. The linens had accumulated some dirt, on their fringes, which tended to flip off into the dirt when Pantagathus was asleep, in his place, beside the building, with the colloquy of cicadas, who were silenced at the whim of the vas, and also with the wet leaves, making contact. Pantagathus was to go to the stream and clean the linens, with brevity, and then he was to come back to the building and make the lumber an alit resource. It would be a resource for the cook, who was Pantagathus, and a resource for vitriol. It was to be a resource of hypnotizability.

The fish were to be cooked, in the fire pit, and the linens were to dry, strewn out by the chamomile, in the garden; Pantagathus was to lie on the bundled sacks. None of this had been conceived. It was slow and elevating in the cognizant spirals of mind. Tavis, the heretic, was plucking a few strings. It was randomized plucking of fingers. There was no rhythm. He had been listening to the oscillations, which occurred in the in between notes, and which many times broke strings. It wobbled and Tavis, the heretic, brought it back to tune, with gaiety and with Pantagathus sitting up and against the building, beside the building, where he slept, and Pantagathus was on his linens. The linens were folded. They had not been washed for months. Pantagathus tucked the linens beneath his arm, and exited the rhapsodic exclamation, an action, which would take place once more in sixty minutes. The linens had to dry, strewn out by the chamomile, in the garden, on their fringes, which tended to be the only parts in want of a clean; the linens were to be collated with the cold water, which was in a murmur at the whim of the mountain, and also with the wet leaves, making contact. Pantagathus was at the stream and had begun to clean the linens, with brazen fay, and then he came back to the building and did not make the lumber an alit riposte. Rather, he had lain the linens, strewn by the chamomile, and went inside to gather the soap. It would be a rigmarole for the priest, who was Pantagathus, and a rigmarole for virility. It was to be a rigmarole of affability—the small fish, in two hours were cooked and were eaten; the small fish did not have a bad lot; there was no bad taste—and the clean Pantagathus, who had not soaped in three months, was lying in the place he had been lying, by the side of the building, where he slept, and drying in the dryness of Kosmidion, in the hot season. The stavrouli, which Pantagathus had taken off, and then pocketed, and then put in the drawer in the kitchen had stayed off for the hours in between then and the drying in the dryness. He had not touched the stavrouli in that amount of time, and then, hours before the surfacing of the idea to wash the linens, Pantagathus took the stavrouli and put it on his neck, where it belonged, and where it was then, with Pantagathus lying in his place, beside the building, where he slept. Tavis, the heretic, was plucking a few stings. A rhythm had become manifest. It started and lulled. He had been arriving at and relinquishing sustainability, which occurred in between each pluck, and which many times broke hearts. It wobbled and Tavis, the heretic, brought it back too soon, because Pantagathus was cooking the small fish, which did not have a bad lot, and because there was no bad taste. They were quite deliberate, in their feigning in and out of reliability, from the stream and from the bath waters of Pantagathus and Tavis, the heretic—all of which spectred.

July had become August, and the chamomile was to be harvested. Pantagathus examined the chamomile. The buds were fat on the Streptophyta. They were to be yummy. One smelled the pungent herb, close the garden. Closer the Streptophyta, it was intoxicating. There was chamomile, which had been brought from Yves Albatrois, maker of guitars. It was brought with the guitar strings, which found themselves on the guitar of Tavis, the heretic. It was the chamomile from Yves Albatrois, maker of guitars, they were drinking during the first exchange they had had, with supposed hostility. They had their own chamomile, within four hours, which was the remaining length of time the Helios had before its getting bowed over the spherical prismatic. The seemless chromatics shifted; they were viscous. No changes could be made. There was no severance. There were differences—a difference in deviance; a difference in music, which was art, and which was a centerless end of inspiration. The parabolic bends of the vocal chords, which incited the first syllable spoken in hours, were soliloquized.

1923

It had been two days at the homestead, and Panagiotis was working with the heads of sheep. In the two days, following their arrival, the old man gave Panagiotis a break; the work would begin in two days' time, and his time was his until then, to explore the town and meet villagers and create for himself a routine, which would, of course, find its way around the work schedule, in place in the subsequent weeks. The old man had showed Panagiotis the sheep, the day following their arrival, and the sheep were pinned in a small corral, with their feed and with two dogs. The sheep numbered over a hundred. The corral was of moderate size, the dogs of a medium-large build, and Panagiotis could not tell of their pure heritage and considered them the most mixed and voracious accompaniments in town. He had gone into the corral with the old man, and the dog, who was the larger of the two dogs, did bar its teeth and make saliva on the ground, and it was only a small amount of saliva; Panagiotis did not consider himself in danger of the rabies. The larger of the two dogs did bar its teeth, and though the initial introduction between the specimen Canis lupus familiaris and he, Panagiotis, was not very forthcoming, the subsequent days would not be disagreeable to either the specimen Canis lupus familiaris, nor to Panagiotis, with the aid of the old man and his affiliation with the dog, who was an alcoholic. The dog did bar its teeth, and the old man said, "Give him wine. He'll like you after you give him wine." The old man handed over his small wine skin to Panagiotis, who went over to the water bowl of the dog and poured out the water and refilled the bowl with the wine. The dog did not resist to the approaching and alien person. The dog knew well what was in the skin and there was no problem with the alien going ahead and enabling the larger of the two dogs to hit the skins. The head count was made of the sheep and the dog was drinking wine. It was a typical day at the corrals, the day Panagiotis had full control of the workable aspects of the corral—the feed and the water—and in the hot season the head of sheep would be in want of a sheer, for the temperament and for the commodity. In the two days, in between the arrival in the town and the first day of working the corral, Panagiotis did make an acquaintance out of that dog, who was named Zito, and who was to be the father of a litter of dogs, who were to arrive within one month. The mother dog was residing in the shed, and after a couple of days of drink and raillery, Zito allowed Panagiotis to approach the small, wooden house, within which lay Zuny, who was rather along in her litter. The day was short, at the corrals. In all of actuality, the work at the farm was well taken care of by the plantation workers and the servants, who numbered few, and who were entitled and considered a part of the familial organism of the homestead, in Levantant ways and in matter of fact. Following the short day at the corral, Panagiotis went back to the main house, where there was a courtyard, in which all had eaten the afternoon of their arrival, and where a small area was located, the area called the laboratory, where the family experimented with botanics and with parental philosophia, both of which were met with success, and in monumentality; the courtyard, in which all had eaten the afternoon of their arrival, was located in the corner of the main building, which was shaped like a capital L. On the opposite side of the main building was the laboratory.

Children, the nieces and nephews of Santeia and Harito, danced and sniveled at each other. Panagiotis watched, while sitting in the laboratory. The hybrid Plantæ were in four respective locations, in the small garden, to the side of which Panagiotis looked at the nieces and nephews, with placated eyes and with a glass of wine or whiskey, from the distillery, because it was a determined life and it was a finite life and it was a precious life, of which all were a part and, in the plantation fields, men and women worked, with their children, and there was a difference only in the time of day the dry meats were eaten and in the location of the wine being drinked; all of the wine was stored in casks, beneath the main house. There were no locks. The homestead was rather separate from the rest of the town, and those who lived in the area where the homestead was located worked for the homestead and had full access to the casks for standard usage and siphoning. Panagiotis did enjoy the wine. He had been into the cellar two times and he enjoyed the heaviness of the cellar and also the sizes of the casks. They were quite large and nobody would say otherwise, unless they were drinking the drink, which came from the distillery, which was further northwards and closer the corral, and the abundance of which was housed in the distillery, too, which did have a lock on its door, contrary to the cellar door and most doors in the household. Panagiotis was having a drink, in the laboratory. He clutched his glass. Around the house, Santeia was using the W.C. The baby did miscarry. She kicked dirt onto the white embryonic. Panagiotis saw her when she rounded the corner of the capital L, and she looked well.

"You look well," said Panagiotis.

"I am not well."

"What is at hand?"

"It is of no importance."

"Sit with me and drink."

"Okay." She sat at the chair, opposite the table, at which Panagiotis had been sitting.

"The nieces and nephews are a rancorous lot."

"They are a rancorous lot. They are a watchful lot."

"Go ahead and drink something," said Panagiotis.

Santeia had a drink from the bottle. "I am not going to drink much. The girls in the house are preparing lamb for the evening. I don't want to drink too much before the dinner. I'll drink at the dinner and you can fret me then."

"Okay, I'll fret you then."

"Do you need to go with me to the lemons, or do you have such abandon?"

"Let's get the lemons," said Panagiotis. He had arisen with his glass, and he took a drink, following which Panagiotis and Santeia walked a little further northwards, towards to the distillery and towards the lemons, to harvest a few lemons for the meal of lamb and potatoes. "How are you enjoying the town?"

"It is advantageous, being here. I have not been here, in my years. I was in Constantinople, which was much different, and the town, here, is advantageous, more advantageous than Constantinople even."

"How do you say that?"

"One does actions for the good of one's own. One cooks their own foods and makes their babies and the families are the first to touch the baby, when it is making its pains."

"It is an advantageous town. That is a valid way of putting it, when you say it like that—food and babies. It makes sense. Constantinople was advantageous, too."

"Not like Kassitera."

"The water is better in Kassitera," said Panagiotis.

"The water is better in Kassitera," said Santeia. They had reached the lemons. Panagiotis pulled three from a lemon tree and Santeia pulled a couple from a different lemon tree. They were walking back to the main house, in the homestead, with the lemons and with the homesickness. The water was better in Kassitera. The two did agree. That the water of Kassitera was apt for larva upon stillness, in a shorter time, and listeria upon stillness, in a shorter time, was not a problem for the two, Panagiotis and Santeia. They did not know the water in Kassitera was different. The lesser nieces and nephews approached Panagiotis and Santeia. The kitchen, which was off of the inside corner of the capital L, was busied with girls. The old man sat at the table in the courtyard. He had given Panagiotis the key to the distillery shed. Panagiotis went further northwards, towards the lemons and the corral. The maladroit rooftop of the distillery shed was sullen, in the sublimation, which was more prevalent once inside the distillery shed. Panagiotis went inside and siphoned off a jug of whiskey. Panagiotis relocked the shed door after he had gone inside the distillery and had siphoned off the glass jug of whiskey. He walked back to the courtyard, in the corner of the capital L. Two glasses of whiskey were poured for the old man and he, and then Stefangianopoulou joined them.

Stefangianopoulou said, "How has been your day?"

"Not bad," Panagiotis said. "Not bad at all. How has been your day, Stefangianopoulou?"

"The fields were well and we manicured an area."

"The heads of sheep were, too, well. We drank."

"You and who else were at the corral?"

"It was Zito and I, who were drinking."

"Zito? Have I yet to meet him?"

"He is the four-legged quadruped. He is the candor."

"He is the sheep dog."

"He is in your sights."

The evening time and the lamb and potatoes were brought to the inside courtyard of the capital L, by the girls and by the Hypnos. The nieces and nephews were running and screaming. The children danced and sniveled at each other. Panagiotis watched, from the temporality and from behind the stone partition, in between the street and the courtyard of the capital L. Their rightfulness was the Manx.

2017

The snow had been on the ground for an hour and a half, and it was still finding its way down to the Newfoundlander floor and the hill, in the westward direction. Pete Tsiminis had awoken and had looked out of his window, with the reconstrued skeleton and with the sack of fire wood, down below his window, on the floor of the backyard, which was covered with five inches of precipitation; the sack of fire wood was near covered, in entirety. One saw the gray outlines of the sack of fire wood, and then the eyes were taken into the Betulaceæ, which backed the Tsiminis home, and which, too, was taken by the aspro climactic. It was a day for the hill. The weekend, once more, had arrived. Pete Tsiminis had missed school, over the week, for multiple reasons, one of which was the incapacitation of Jonathon, who was to stay indoors and heal, and who also, in four hours, was to find his way to the hill, with the ditch at the bottom of the hill and with the kids, who, too, would reside in the wintertime revels.

The breakfast of toast and eggs had been eaten. Pete Tsiminis was well rested, and he was going to need the revived energy, which had accumulated over the frigid night, in the pursuit of the hill slope and the velocity. Pete

Tsiminis went into the garage. The sled, which had been made years prior, and which was composed of two by fours and the two disparaged pieces of metal, which would otherwise have been parts to the fire place hearth the father of Pete Tsiminis managed to apprehend with forty dollars and with rended phonics, had a rope tied to its runners, used to pull the sled in the direction of vagrancy. Pete Tsiminis was awake, and he had clothed himself in his long johns and heavy socks; and then, he slid on his snow pants and his sweatshirt, following which the jacket of volume was assumed, all of which had taken Pete Tsiminis into the garage, to the boots, which he put onto his feet, and then to the Jonathon household, in subsequence. It was eleven o'clock A.M. Jonathon answered the door. Pete Tsiminis put his sled in the foliage, on the right-hand side of the door, facing the harbor, which was westwards. Pete Tsiminis and Jonathon were to ready themselves, and then they were to make the right out of the Jonathon household and onto Basalt Road, and then once more a right onto Piccadilly Street, which would take them eastwards, towards the fork in the road and towards the hill, in contiguity.

Pete Tsiminis had been ready, and, sitting at the kitchen table in the house of the family of Jonathon, he had begun to sweat. Jonathon was near finished. "—and then, we're going to go to the hill to watch the people sled down the hill," said Pete Tsiminis to the mother of Jonathon. She did not know Jonathon was to partake in the hill raucousness, nor was she to find out about the incorporation of Jonathon in the hill raucousness. Rather, she sat at the kitchen table, with her tea, and spoke to Pete Tsiminis, whose face had begun to moisten in the heavy clothes and in the heat of the house of the family of Jonathon; Jonathon was ready.

"Bye, mom."

"Bye, sweetie."

"Bye, Mrs. A—"

"Bye, Pete. Stay safe, Jonathon, and don't put stress on your ankle."

"Bye, mom."

"Bye, you two."

Pete Tsiminis collected his sled, made of the two by fours and the disparaged pieces of metal for runners, and Jonathon had gone into the garage and retrieved his sled, which was made from the sled factory, they had established. They gave to their saunter. Basalt Road was taken, and, into Piccadilly Street, the snowfall had thickened beneath their feet. That was no problem. It was all appropriate. The hill was of importance. The ankle of Jonathon was not of so much concern. It had been bagged, in a garbage bag. Jonathon had tied yarn around the ankle. It did not look as if it would repel water when it was finished, and Jonathon applied tape to the ankle; it looked better and more water repellant. The hill came into their sights. It was well moddled with white. People were straggling at the top of the hill. A couple of people were on their way down, on their respective vessels; they hit the divot and Pete Tsiminis and Jonathon saw each of them propel into the ditch, where it was, too, fulsome in its collected precipitation. They mounted the hill, each of them, Pete Tsiminis and Jonathon, in apprehension of their sleds; kids were atop the hill and the kids beckoned hello, to which also Pete Tsiminis and Jonathon bid hello. They were excitable. The ankles of Pete Tsiminis and Jonathon and just as well any of the kids at the top of that hill were no different than the others. They were all complex; they were all vulnerable. Pete Tsiminis set his runners into the snow, at the top of the hill. "Watch your ankle," he said. "Dweeb." He sped down the hill.

"Watch your ass," Jonathon said, as Pete Tsiminis pushed off with his hands. Jonathon mounted his sled, which was like a contact lens.

Pete Tsiminis went down the hill, fast. The hill, the road, off of which was the fork in the road, and the view over the Betulaceæ dematerialized—all found its way back into actuality, at the bottom of the hill, with the jostled divot and with the airtime; Pete Tsiminis landed in the ditch, where he got up on his booted feet and started to dance, his arms and his legs akimbo; Jonathon, with his ankle and with his toiled lustre, got air and landed in the ditch. He got up and did the chicken leg. Pete Tsiminis started to play the drum set. It was a Zeppelin tune and it was pretty stack. They mounted the hill, once more, for a second run; Pete Tsiminis said, "How was the ankle?"

"What ankle?" said Jonathon.

"Have you lost your ankle? The one with the tic-tac-toe and dots, Monsieur Menagerie."

"Oui, Pete Tsimounis. I have lost my ankle."

"Good. Down you go," said Pete Tsiminis. They were at the top of the hill, and once more they did their run, first Jonathon, with his sled like the contact lens from the sled factory, they had established, and then Pete Tsiminis, with his sled, made of wood and scrap metal; they hit the divot, they got air, they landed in the ditch. They got up and hit the scuzzy ribbon, and Pete Tsiminis got on his drum set and finished strong with a Cristopher Cross tune nobody knew and everybody knew, because it was that time, Jonathon, to go home and veg with the steel leg.

"You do have a steel leg," said Pete Tsiminis.

"I don't have a steel leg. It's not a steel leg. It's not made of steel. It's—"

"You are the steel leg."

"You are the iron gate."

Pete Tsiminis said, "You are the aluminum foil."

Jonathon said, "You are the titanium monkey."

Pete Tsiminis said, "Let's go home and eat plums."

The two acquaintances made home. They had walked through the high snow of Piccadilly Street. Jonathon said, "Are you upset I called you the titanium monkey?"

Pete Tsiminis said, "I didn't mind."

The house of the family of Jonathon accepted them well. They brushed off the snow before entering the house, through the garage, where Jonathon replaced his sled, and his parents were not going to find out about his sledding that morning, because it had been subtle and it had been genteel.

1453

Tavis, the heretic, was preparing the wheat Yves Albatrois, maker of guitars, had requested as compensation for the guitar strings and the other supplies he sent along, many of times. In all of actuality, Yves Albatrois, maker of guitars, had much wheat, at his plantation, which was full of crop of all types. It was more of a principle, Tavis, the heretic, preparing and delivering the wheat to Yves Albatrois, maker of guitars, upon arrival at the festivities, and Tavis, the heretic, was not against the gesture. He enjoyed the principle of principle and he enjoyed the company of Yves Albatrois, maker of guitars, even more so than principle, and he was enjoying himself the day prior the commencement of the festivities, preparing the wheat into two large sacks. Pantagathus was sitting at the fire pit. He had noted it was an action of no affectation. The two sacks of wheat were not much beside the plantation in its fullness. He did not say anything to Tavis, the heretic, in regards to such a notion. The wheat was to be prepared, and Pantagathus was to carry the sacks of wheat in the former half of the walk northwards, towards the homestead of Yves Albatrois, maker of guitars, and Tavis, the heretic, was to carry the sacks of wheat the latter half of the walk northwards, towards the homestead of

Yves Albatrois, maker of guitars, and the sacks would both be carried by one, in each half of their journey, for balance sake and for the sake of symmetry.

Tavis, the heretic, was binding the wheat into compact bushels. The two sacks were to contain more wheat in that way, with the binds and with the stratagem. It was not so much the wheat, of which Pantagathus was thinking, as much as it was the festivities, which were to commence in twenty-four hours.

Tavis, the heretic, was, too, thinking about the festivities and not the wheat, with such immediacy; he was musing on the peculiarities of the festivities—the mannish drink and the song, which would ensue over the following seventy-two hours of festivity and renascence. The sacks were near capacity.

Tavis, the heretic, bound the sacks at their necks. He carried them to the side of the building, beside the place, where Pantagathus had slumber in the evenings and, sometimes, in the afternoon, with the chamomile in the vein streams. The sacks of wheat were finished. Pantagathus arose from his seat beside the fire pit. He approached the sacks of wheat. Tavis, the heretic, was sorting the two sacks, in the way they were not to fall over on their sides. "The wheat is ready and in their sacks."

"I see that."

"We will leave for the homestead of Yves tomorrow morning, following a bath, if it is in need."

"Are they heavy?" said Pantagathus, referring to the sacks of wheat.

"They are not lightweight."

"Will the journey be a struggle, with the sacks of wheat?"

"Of course not."

"Of course not. Why would the journey be a struggle, with the sacks of wheat?"

"It will not be a struggle, with the sacks of wheat."

"I have gathered that the journey will not be a struggle, with the sacks of wheat."

"Will you gather your grapes. I am a bit in need of a bite to eat."

"One minute and I will return with a plate of grapes." Pantagathus went inside the small building and retrieved a plate. He went around the building, to the side of the building with the grape vine and with the thorns. The plate of grapes was composed. He went back around, towards the front of the building, with the chamomile and with the fire pit. Tavis, the heretic, accepted the plate of grapes, and then he thanked Pantagathus, with a stark monophthong.

"They are—they are so gracious. They are ours. They are—they are so sagacious. They are so supplicant."

"I am glad you enjoy the plate of grapes."

"Sit, Pantagathus. Sit."

Pantagathus sat on the chair, which was beside the unlit fire pit.

"Are you excitable for the festivities?"

"Of course. I have not seen a human face in months, Tavis, the heretic."

"There will be much drink and many girls."

"I do hesitate in such pursuits."

"That is unworthy."

Pantagathus said, "What is uncouth is unworthy. Tavis, the heretic, I enjoy easy temperament."

"As do I, Pantagathus."

"It will be hot in the festivities. Such drink and such a numerous many girls will contribute to the volatility."

"It is hot in the homestead of Yves Albatrois."

"What is it like?"

"He has got a basement, with a particular ingenuity. He has created a jet of sorts and the jet goes through the basement of its own accord, with the wind and physics."

"The basement would be hot otherwise."

"Indeed, the basement was hot in the years prior his ingenuity."

"Will you have your residence in that basement, heathen?"

"Yes, I will reside in the basement much of the time throughout the festivities. The question is, however, of importance. Are you to have much drink at the festivities?"

"I will drink."

"Perhaps, it is best to refine the question in the terms of what is to be drinked, in which case I would ask are you to have the mannish drink?"

"The mannish drink?"

"The mannish drink. It is a tasteful drink. It is a mannish drink. It is a tasty mannish drink."

"I do not know of such a drink, of such mannishness and tastefulness, in the stead of your raillery."

"Do you need to drink the mannish drink?"

"Do I need to drink the mannish drink. The mannish drink is mannish and tasty. Why would I not want the mannish drink?"

"Does the mannish drink call to you?"

"Of what is the mannish drink made?"

"It is made of a peculiar syrup, which grows on the plantation of Yves Albatrois, maker of guitars. Which preceded which, however, the syrup or the guitars, is another question, as far as Yves in concerned."

"Are there particular effects?"

"Yes, there are effects," said Tavis, the heretic, who raised his eyebrow and ate grapes. The optics of Pantagathus, in the perpendicularity, with Tavis, the heretic, in the foreground, were staggered into the coordinate points, which would take Pantagathus to the homestead of Yves Albatrois, maker of guitars, and which would take Tavis, the heretic, to the homestead of Yves Albatrois, maker of guitars, and it was to make another plane another plane.

1923

Panagiotis was giving the heads of sheep feed. It was the morning time and the morning time was the feed time for the heads of sheep. The routine had fallen in, around the workday, which was what the old man had suggested happen, and which was what had happened, in the very early days of the residence in Kassitera. The breakfast had been eaten. It was of bread and cheese, from the village. The corral had inside it Panagiotis, who did have a wine skin with him, and who did pour out the water from the bowl of Zito and replace the water with wine. Panagiotis was to refill the water bowl, upon his leaving the corral. The wine was depleted with near immediacy.

The smaller of the two dogs, Zuny, who was rather large at the point in her litter, was lying in the barn, and Panagiotis took a look inside of the barn and Zuny was lying on her side. Her legs were in the direction of the head of sheep and the barn door. Her head was to the left-hand side of Panagiotis, and Zuny was having to respire with a moderate effort. Panagiotis stayed in the barn for a few minutes. He watched Zuny and patted her head. Zito approached and they were a tripartite idyll, for a minute. Panagiotis went out into the corral, with the heads of sheep and with the feed. He dispersed of a plentiful amount of feed, in the four feed benches, in the four places of the corral, with equal distance, in between each of the feed benches. The water was refilled in the water benches. Panagiotis had gone and received the water from the cistern, which was two dozen steps closer the main house. It was about halfway to the main house, and Panagiotis needed to see Zuny and give Zito drink prior receiving the water from the cistern. It was early in the morning; and there was no want for rapidity.

For a while longer, Panagiotis stayed in the corral, with Zito, drinking wine. The wine skin was depleted. Panagiotis went back to the main house and went into the inside corner courtyard of the house in its capital L. In all of reality, it was more so the gamma, or the Greek Γ, when coming from the direction of the corral and the cistern, beside which was the distillery and the lemons, and just as well many an abundance of fruits, which fed the family, who resided in the main building, and which also fed the plantation workers, who were of importance. Harito was sitting in the capital L courtyard. He, too, was drinking his breakfast wine.

Harito said, "Stefangianopoulou is working on his invention, or Stefangianopoulou is working on my invention, if that is how you need to see it."

"What is he inventing, peculiar as he is?"

"It has something to do with the thresh."

"Don't they all have something to do with the thresh?"

"In all probability."

"How did you sleep?" said Panagiotis.

Harito said, "I slept well. How was your morning? How were the heads of sheep, Good Shepard?"

"The heads were well. Zito and I were drinking the wine. He can drink, that scat. It is like he has no inhibition."

"None have anything of the sort, Panagiotis."

"You won the bet," said Panagiotis. "That counts as a bit of inhibition, as I see it. Perhaps not an immediate inhibition. It is inhibition."

"Yes, I won the bet."

"You kept your stamps."

"I kept my stamps."

Panagiotis said, "I may ask you for a stamp. I need to send a letter to my mother and her home town. It may be where she is headed. She may receive my letter, with luck."

"You can have a stamp, as well as all the kuruş."

"Many thanks," said Panagiotis. "Then, I can bribe the children and they can like me, like I bribed the dog, Zito, to like me."

"Do you need to go to the barn with me, to lambaste Stefangianopoulou, or is it just my mirth?"

"Let us go to see Stefangianopoulou." Harito arose, with his wine. Panagiotis and Harito went to the barn, closer the laboratory. In was the only place, which had a bit of privacy, and the barn with the distillery was not appropriate for the invention pursuit, as per the smell and as per the lack of area. They knocked on the barn door, and it opened outwards, towards Harito and Panagiotis. An upside-down wheel barrow, made of wood, was supporting a wheel of a wagon; the wheel was a spare wheel and it was lying on its side, flat and atop the wheel barrow, and there were strings and pegs in the spare wheel, upwards.

"An ingenious machine—"

"Do not criticize, Harito," said Stefangianopoulou. "It is not finished."

"I do not criticize. It will be well constructed and sold to seamstresses everywhere."

The small window in the eastward wall of the barn allowed in the cadence of the morning and illuminated dust motes. They sustained their Levantine. Stefangianopoulou walked through the cadence and the dust motes. He picked up his bottle of wine and drank a small drink from the bottle. Everybody was drinking; everybody was wanton, because it was Kassitera and Constantinople was a millennium bygone.

Panagiotis moved to touch the thresh. "Is it—"

"Don't touch it. It is not held together by anything. Not yet."

"What will it do, Stefangianopoulou?"

"It will expedite the germination of crops."

"Does it require water?"

"It requires water."

"Is it like the automobile?" said Harito.

"If I were to have an automobile I would not be making this invention. If I were to have an automobile I would take Santeia back to Eptadendros, for the evening."

"I won the bet, Stefangianopoulou," Harito said. "Santeia is out of reach."

"I would not be in the possession of an automobile, anyway. There is no reason to get emotional."

"There is no automobile in this town," said Harito. "I doubt an automobile will ever gain entrance into this town."

"The invention might change that. Popular people might come when they hear about my invention."

"It is my invention, Stefangianopoulou, lest we forget."

"Forget you, wop." Stefangianopoulou went back to his invention. It was the invention of Harito, if one were to be so peculiar; it was Kassitera. Nobody really doubted anything.

1453

It was the morning of the festivities. Early in the morning, Pantagathus had awoken to the arpeggio of the Ornethura. They were in flight. It was the morning of the festivities. They did not know about the festivities. They were Ornethura. They were in flight and the arpeggio of the Ornethura was, to Pantagathus, a hypnœsis, which was not separate from baseless celebration. The Ornethura procured the Helios into wakefulness, or the Helios in its arch was the initiative of the Ornethura. Either way, Pantagathus had awoken in the early morning, and it was the morning of the festivities, which were to be held at the homestead of Yves Albatrois, maker of guitars, for the next sevety-two hours. Pantagathus and Tavis, the heretic, were to commence in their travels, within four hours. The wheat, which had been put into sacks, by the labor of Tavis, the heretic, was above the head of Pantagathus when he had been lying down in his place by the building, where the linens, which were now clean and dry, were, and where he slept. The wheat, which had been put into sacks, by the labor of Tavis, the heretic, was on the right-hand side of Pantagathus, who was sitting up and against the building; he was watching the chromatic ascendancy.

He went into the building and retrieved a half loaf of bread, which he cut in twain, into two even halves, down the middle, for the breakfasts of he, Pantagathus, and Tavis, the heretic, both of which were to eat in equal amounts, for the travels northwards, towards the homestead of Yves Albatrois, maker of guitars.

Tavis, the heretic, roused from sleep upon the door being opened from the outside, by Pantagathus. He said not a word, and he put his feet on the wooden floor boards. Pantagathus was outside, once more, with his half of the remaining bread and with half of the remainder of the cheese; he sat and ate his breakfast, and then Tavis, the heretic, came outside in the high indium. "A pleasant day," said Tavis, the heretic.

"Indeed, a pleasant day. It is the day of the festivities, Tavis, the heretic."

"It is a pleasant day for the raucous and the vagrant," said Tavis, the heretic. He had in his hands his half of the remaining loaf of bread and also his piece of cheese. He sat at the fire pit. "I do not want to arrive too early at the homestead of Yves. We will leave in two hours at the latest."

"I am glad. Also, I need to bring the remaining wine into the considerations," said Pantagathus. "I would like to bring some of our wine, for good purposes."

"Bring wine. In the latter half of the travels, you and I will switch effects, wheat and wine to the other."

"Do you have wine?"

"It is inside. Let me get the wine." Tavis, the heretic, came back outside with a bottle of wine. "It is not the last of the wine. We have two jugs remaining."

Pantagathus said, "Let us finish this wine. There is not much remaining in the bottle. We can prepare for the travels, afterwards." Pantagathus was handed the bottle of wine. He uncorked the bottle and drinked a small bit of the wine. A rose streak went down his chin, which was hairy; the wine, which had streaked down his hairy chin was visible, even in the ascendancy, which was near full illumined.

Tavis, the heretic, said. "Is there a leak or are you a sloppy drinker?"

"Neither," said Pantagathus. "I am an exogenesis."

"Keep the wine in your mouth."

"Keep the foolishness in yours, heathen."

Tavis, the heretic, said. "I don't need to ruin the upholstery."

"I will do it for you. I'm in the horrible notion. I'm sitting on it."

Tavis, the heretic, spoke to his right ear, "It is the kind of people like this who are going to end this thing." Tavis, the heretic, was handed the bottle of wine, which was near depleted, and he finished the wine, within five minutes.

The early morning had become the mid-morning, and Tavis, the heretic, took the sacks of wheat onto his shoulders, and he and Pantagathus started northwards, towards the homestead of Yves Albatrois, maker of guitars, and all was cordial. The travels took Pantagathus and Tavis, the heretic, past the rivulet, where they bathed, and where they fished for the small fish, who were, as far as Pantagathus was concerned, volatile. He had eaten three fish of the same outstanding taste. None, in the recent two months, had become manifest. The travels were two hours of walking, through the forests of Kosmidion, until one arrived at a road, which was perpendicular the route walked by Pantagathus and Tavis, the heretic, and when the walker reached the perpendicular road, a right-hand turn was to be made and five hundred paces forwards, the homestead of Yves Albatrois, maker of guitars, was found on the left-hand side and northward side of the road, with the plantations and with the building. It had been an hour walk and few stops had been made en route towards the perpendicular road. The only stops, which were made, were made to have a drink of wine from the wine skins, and the wine from the wine skins, in the latter half of the travels, was near depleted. Tavis, the heretic, had handed the sacks of wheat to Pantagathus, and Pantagathus handed the jugs of wine to Tavis, the heretic. The halfway point of the travels was cued by a shattered pine tree. It lay splayed, in two directions. Beside the shattered pine tree, the exchange had been made; Pantagathus and Tavis, the heretic, did continue forwards towards the perpendicular road, and there was jocularity and tachycardia. The perpendicular road was met, by the two, Pantagathus and Tavis, the heretic, and the right-hand turn was made, and then, five hundred paces later, the two, Pantagathus, with the sacks of wheat on his shoulders, and Tavis, the heretic, with the jugs of wine, and also his guitar tied to his back, with a rope, approached the homestead of Yves Albatrois, maker of guitars, and mounted his steps; Tavis, the heretic, walked into the house, which was three floors in height and spackled. Tavis, the heretic, was not lying. It was an excellent place for the festivities. Pantagathus, prior walking into the house, put the sacks of wheat on the outside floor, which was waxy.

There were few people in the house. A few girls were flitting in and out of rooms, on the first floor of the house; Yves Albatrois, maker of guitars, was in the kitchen. Tavis, the heretic, went over to the kitchen table and slapped him, with ease, on the shoulder. The girls were lying table clothes on tables and couches and chairs. The rugs were to be moved and rolled. They were to lean against the walls of their respective rooms. There was no need for rugs in the festivities. In the rug's stead, the waxy floor was to be the matter, and also the dancing and drink, which was to occur in the respective rooms and on the floors.

Tavis, the heretic, said, "A pleasant morning."

Yves Albatrois, maker of guitars, said, "A pleasant morning. It is the morning of the festivities."

"It is, indeed, and this is Pantagathus, the priest, from Constantinople." Tavis, the heretic, put the jugs of wine on the kitchen table, which had been affixed with a table cloth not the usual and stylish table cloth, which, Pantagathus gathered, was of the table, in normality. This table cloth was practical and was meant to sustain mistakes.

Yves Albatrois, maker of guitars, nodded his head. "A pleasant day, Pantagathus, the priest, from Constantinople."

"A pleasant day, Yves Albatrois."

"Yves will do."

"Of course," said Pantagathus. "It is a gallant house. The festivities will be gallant, in equanimity, if Tavis, the heretic, does relay of its inclinations, with accuracy."

"I do not know Tavis, the heretic, to lie," said Yves Albatrois, maker of guitars.

Pantagathus said, "Neither do I know of Tavis, the heretic, to do what his name indicates. It all seems an inconstancy, and this is your house, Yves, maker of guitars.

What does that mean to you? The festivities will answer my question; there is no need to reply."

Yves Albatrois, maker of guitars, turned to Tavis, the heretic, and said, "Do you two need anything to eat?"

"Why not?" said Tavis, the heretic. "We have been walking for two hours, through the wood. Do you need anything to eat Pantagathus? Get us something, Yves, anything."

"We have the plantation. There are many fruits, and also bread if you were so inclined."

Tavis, the heretic, pulled out the chair from the kitchen table. "We will ask the girls to get a plate of fruit for us."

Yves Albatrois, maker of guitars, said to Pantagathus, "There is bread over there, in the big cabinet. Go over there and take a loaf of bread and come over here to sit."

Pantagathus opened the big cabinet, and there were loaves of bread and there were jars of macaroni and a few potatoes, on the shelf in front of Pantagathus. Also, the jars of chamomile and coffee were to the left-hand side of the big cabinet, and dried beans and herbs were in jars, too. Pantagathus took out a loaf of bread, behind which were dried fruits. He assumed his place at the kitchen table, and a girl, who was wearing a long skirt came into the kitchen, with a linen and with her hair styled to the sides.

Yves Albatrois, maker of guitars, said, "Patri, get some fruit from the garden and bring over a plate of fruit. Thanks."

"Of course, baba."

"She's a good girl and my youngest."

Patri came back into the kitchen and put a bunch of grapes and a few strawberries on a plate. Also, she brought in half of a cantaloupe, which she cleaned and, too, included on the plate of fruit. "Here you are, baba and friends."

"Thanks, Patri," said Pantagathus. "I will get glasses for the wine." Pantagathus got up from his chair. People walked into the kitchen. The eyes of Patri widened. She had been standing in front of Pantagathus when he stood up from the kitchen table, to retrieve the wine glasses.

"You are so much taller than you looked sitting down," said Patri.

Pantagathus retrieved the glasses, which were, too, included in the big cabinet. "Taller? Much taller or a little taller?"

"Much taller," said Patri. "You are much taller than I guessed when you were sitting down."

Pantagathus sat back down at the kitchen table. Tavis, the heretic, started his hysterics, "I want a fork. I want a fork—a fork. I want a fork. I want a fork."

Patri said, "I will get you a fork." She got forks for everybody, who was sitting around the kitchen table. All ate the fruit, and the fruit was depleted within twenty minutes. It was high noon, and lamb was to be cooked for the people, who were already at the homestead of Yves Albatrois, maker of guitars, and who were few, in number; the lamb had been cooked and eaten well, and there was some lamb remaining for the individuals, who were to arrive, with immediacy.

The meal was finished, and the girls cleaned the tables. One table was outside, and the three, Pantagathus, Tavis, the heretic, and Yves Albatrois, maker of guitars, sat at the outside table, and the girls sat at the inside kitchen table where the three, Pantagathus, Tavis, the heretic, and Yves Albatrois, maker of guitars, had sat and had eaten the plate of fruit, a couple of hours earlier. All three of the males were sitting at the outside table, and Yves Albatrois, maker of guitars, said, "The festivities will last for three days."

Tavis, the heretic, said, "Indeed."

"You will need your own bedrooms."

"Quite," said Tavis, the heretic.

"Follow me and we will find room for the two of you, on the top floor of the house." Yves Albatrois, maker of guitars, led the two, Pantagathus and Tavis, the heretic, into the house and past the kitchen table, which had been cleaned off of plates and silverware, and which was draped with the practical linens. The tripartition went back towards the front of the house, where the two travelers had entered hours earlier, and, walking towards the front door, Yves Albatrois, maker of guitars, made a right-hand turn, in through a door, which was a staircase, and brought the two travelers to the second floor of the house, in its colloquy. On the second floor, Yves Albatrois, maker of guitars, said, "There is a staircase here, which brings you up to one side of the third floor, and there is a staircase here, which brings you up to the other side of the third floor. That staircase is for you, Pantagathus. Your bedroom is at the top of those stairs, to the right-hand side, and if one were to walk further down the hallway and past your bedroom door, a corridor, on your right-hand side would take you to the opposite side of the third floor, because this house is sick."

"It wants the salt, is that what you are telling me, Yves?" said Pantagathus.

"It needs you to lie down."

"I will do as so, Yves. Thanks."

"A pleasant day, Pantagathus."

"It is the day of the festivities."

"I will see you upon your reentrance," said Yves Albatrois, maker of guitars, and Pantagathus went up the staircase on the far side of the second floor and found his bedroom; Tavis, the heretic, had done the same, in the staircase closer the area of the formalities. Both of the travelers slept for a couple of hours, because the festivities were to begin, and because the house was tainted.

Tavis, the heretic, walked into the bedroom of Pantagathus. It had been a couple of hours. Pantagathus was not asleep. He was awake, with a subtle easiness, and put his feet on the floor. "This house has many bedrooms," said Tavis, the heretic.

"It does," said Pantagathus. "Did you sleep? How was your sleep?"

"I slept like that which we have eaten."

"The lamb?"

"Yes, the lamb. I slept like the lamb. How did you sleep? Did you sleep?"

"This bedroom is a sleeper's bedroom."

"It is your bedroom. It is your room. I can tell by the embroidery."

"What about the embroidery?"

"It's that way."

"It's what way?'

"Is it all the way over here?"

"Tavis, the heretic, are you a considerable flooby?"

"Quite. Come downstairs. The visitors are beginning to arrive. I looked out my window and saw maybe fifteen or twenty people arrive."

"I can hear them."

"You can hear them."

Pantagathus got out of bed and put on his shoes. Tavis, the heretic, went outside of the room of Pantagathus. Pantagathus came outside of the room, in about sixty seconds, and Tavis, the heretic, had been waiting for him; and then, they went down the staircase together, and further down, to the first floor, where noise was becoming raucous. The sanctuary, which was the room of Pantagathus, in its silence, two hours earlier, was not to be evident for the remainder of the weekend. It was quite over, and Pantagathus was not to hear the silence of the homestead of Yves Albatrois, maker of guitars, for another twenty-four hours, until the visitors, as well as Pantagathus and Tavis, the heretic, and Yves Albatrois, maker of guitars, furrowed into slumber. Tavis, the heretic, went into the kitchen, followed by Pantagathus. The kitchen table was covered with a few items—jugs of wine, two of which were the jugs Pantagathus and Tavis, the heretic, brought with them from the southward direction and from their exclave; a few pieces of meat, a lamb leg and it was hairy; two bottles of clear fluid; and a few sacks of what must have been, to the seeming Pantagathus herbs of a kind or fruit, dried or otherwise, it made little difference, because villages of northern and western Kosmidion had gathered in the homestead of Yves Albatrois, maker of guitars, and they had not stopped arriving—the day of festivities relevant to the visitor, behind whom was another visitor, each of whom had in their hands the clarino, which was to take patrons to the crescendo, to let them back into the graduation of desultory and into degradation. That was the clarino and nobody was to convince Tavis, the heretic, otherwise, not with the mannish drink and not with the caprice. Tavis, the heretic, approached Yves Albatrois, maker of guitars. Pantagathus was behind Tavis, the heretic.

Tavis, the heretic, said, "Let us go downstairs into the basement."

"Why not?" said Yves Albatrois, maker of guitars. "It is time to open the apertures."

Pantagathus stepped aside and Yves Albatrois, maker of guitars, followed by Tavis, the heretic, walked past him, and they went towards the front door; instead of making a right-hand turn, like they had upon ascending the building, with the staircase, the tripartition this time made a left-hand turn, into an adjacent room, with the rug rolled up in the corner of the room, and then another left-hand turn, into a small door, which led down into the basement, using a staircase, which was narrow, and which was senescent. The smell was of soil and it was not unpleasant. Yves Albatrois, maker of guitars, went to the furthest corner of the basement and made his way to the left and moved aside sliding barriers, which opened up a narrow aperture in the wall. It let in little luminescence. He did the same for two other apertures in the two walls, which bordered the outdoors.

"I am to go outside and open the outside parts of these apertures." Yves Albatrois, maker of guitars, went through a small cellar door, in one of the walls, which bordered the outdoors. He said, "Don't leave. We are about to have illumination." The wooden cellar doors opened and the slack outside barriers of the aperture were removed, and luminescence was allowed inside of the basement. A strong vas came into the basement. Yves Albatrois, maker of guitars, came back down the stairs and into the basement. "We have ventilation."

Tavis, the heretic, said, "It's in this place we will have to tousle, over the next three days."

"It is an ingenious contrivance," said Pantagathus.

"I'm going to perform my swallowing action after," said Tavis, the heretic.

Pantagathus went upstairs, through the cellar door, and outside into afternoon Kosmidion, with inquiry.

The apertures were wide on the outside of the house. Pantagathus looked inside one of the apertures. The wideness of aperture narrowed into the small parallelogram Pantagathus had seen in the basement, and which let in the strong vas. The apertures looked handmade. The edges of the aperture, which were in the ground, being that they fed into the basement, were lined with wood, only to differentiate, or perhaps, Pantagathus mused, for æsthetics. The aperture, on the inside was, too, lined with wood. Half of the aperture was in the ground, where Yves Albatrois, maker of guitars, had dug, and there was a small amount of aperture in the wall of the building, for the purposes of torque. Tavis, the heretic, came up and into the Kosmidion outdoors. Yves Albatrois, maker of guitars, followed him. "You have constructed these apertures, as you call them, Yves, I gather?" said Pantagathus.

"I created the apertures, and it was done with ease. The basement wanted ventilation. These arrangements, of importance, the towns in a certain area coming here to the house for the event is not a rarity. It happens twice a year, and years ago, the apertures struck me and it was not a pursuit I was to procrastinate. They have come well into our house."

"Let us go downstairs," Tavis, the heretic, said, "and have wine."

"Go ahead," Yves Albatrois, maker of guitars, said. "We are behind you."

Tavis, the heretic, went downstairs, into the basement, which was in a perpetual vas, and which had been illuminated. The air influxes were quite well in their mechanics, and they were operational to a great extent. Yves Albatrois, maker of guitars, poured wine. There was a jug, which had been filled. Yves Albatrois, maker of guitars, took a drink, and then he handed the jug of wine to Tavis, the heretic, who took a drink of the wine, and who said, "I just performed my swallowing action," and it was good, because the light changed. The three maintained their basement personage, for some minutes, because it was the most comfortable place in the house, and one may well state in all of Kosmidion. The people were heard; they were making noise, walking on the floor, and their screams and raillery were audible to the three, who were in the basement and drinking wine, and who were enthralled by the basement and its cellar door and apertures. "I'm so skinny," said Tavis, the heretic. "I need to be fat. Why couldn't I be big like you," he said, speaking to Yves Albatrois, maker of guitars. "I want to fill the cellar door."

"You want wine," said Yves Albatrois, maker of guitars, who handed the jug of wine back to Tavis, the heretic.

"I am going to get big, Yves," said Tavis, the heretic, "and when I do I'm going to converse with my Ornethura for the next few months."

"You are going to want wine," Yves Albatrois, maker of guitars, said.

"I need chocolate," Tavis, the heretic, said, and they did drink wine for thirty more seconds. They went upstairs, through the staircase, back into the house, where there were visitors preparing not the house but themselves for the festivities; and also were in preparation for the inevitability to illumine.

Two people were sitting at the kitchen table. On the kitchen table were now, as well as the jugs of wine, two of which were the jugs of wine Pantagathus and Tavis, the heretic, had brought with them from the southward direction and their exclave, the pieces of meat, one of which was a lamb leg and it was hairy, and the sacks of herbs and of dry fruit, were two clarinos, upright and on their bells.

A few other people, who had not been in the house earlier, were in the kitchen and helping the girls with this and that. Ten people were in the kitchen, which was large, and most were female. The males were sitting at the kitchen table, with their clarinos. "Yves," said one of the males. "We have arrived for the festivities."

"It is the day of the festivities," said Yves Albatrois, maker of guitars.

"We have brought this wine and also this lamb." The male, with the clarnio at his elbow, slapped the lamb, which was on the kitchen table.

"What was I to do without my lamb," said Yves Albatrois, maker of guitars, "and your perspective?"

"The question is, where is the drink, Yves? I have heard of this drink and I did not consume it the last time you made it. Where is the drink? Let us drink the drink you have made for us and for the festivities."

Tavis, the heretic, said, "The mannish drink, it is mannish and it is tasteful, Mpoulo. It is the mannish drink. It is the mannish and most mannish of mannish drinks. The mannish drink is inevitable and it is fey."

"Have you had the mannish drink, Tavis, the heretic?"

"Yes, I have had the mannish drink. I have had the mannish drink, and it was tasteful, piquant, and it did make foil of me. I would have it no other way, Mpoulo. Are you to drink the mannish drink?"

"Where is the mannish drink? I am to drink it."

"Let us wait some minutes and let the girls leave the kitchen. We will have the mannish drink. It is too hot outside to relax," said Yves Albatrois, maker of guitars. "We will feel rotund, within the hour."

"Rotund?" said Mpoulo.

"The mannish drink," Yves Albatrois, maker of guitars, said, "makes you think as if you were rotund, and then you lie down and rise and you no longer think as if you were rotund."

Tavis, the heretic, said, "What if you were rotund and drinked the mannish drink? Yves, would you think as if you were skinny, and then lie down and rise to no longer think as if you were skinny? Is that what you are insinuating, Yves? Because, Yves, that makes sense."

185

"You will have none of the mannish drink," said Yves Albatrois, maker of guitars.

"I will have the C sharp chord progression on which we have been working in the mannish drink's stead."

"You will have the mannish drink, because I know you are capable in the key of C."

"Get the mannish drink, Yves," said Tavis, the heretic, and Yves Albatrois, maker of guitars, went and got the mannish drink from the shed outside, and brought it back into the kitchen, which was empty except for the five males, Pantagathus, Tavis, the heretic, Yves Albatrois, maker of guitars, Mpoulo, and the other clarino player, who had introduced himself as Moz—with the jugs of wine, two of which had been brought from the southward direction and from the exclave of Pantagathus and Tavis, the heretic; the pieces of meat, one of which was the lamb leg, brought by Mpoulo and Moz, and it was hairy; the bags of herbs and dried fruit; and the two clarinos—and the mannish drink was drinked by Yves Albatrois, maker of guitars, who took six hits of the drink; and then, he passed it to Tavis, the heretic, who drank the mannish drink eight times; he passed it to Pantagathus, who had said, "In how many drinks should I take it," to which Tavis, the heretic, said, "Take it four times, take it six times, take it eight times. Don't take it eleven times. I have not taken it eleven times. Eleven times is much," and Pantagathus took four drinks from the mannish drink; and Mpoulo and Moz took five drinks each, all of the pursuit, in the fifteen minutes following, arrived Pantagathus in a conversation regarding Constantinople and the acoustics of the battle, which had occurred eastwards of his home, and it was, when speaking of the walls and gates and their names, as if another were speaking of the Mesotheitian and the Golden Gate.

"The Golden Gate," Tavis, the heretic, said, "is the gate through which I walked the evening of my exile."

"Very good, Tavis, the heretic," said Mpoulo and all was very cordial, because the afternoon, too, was piquant and people had arrived, in a number close to twenty, from the adjacent towns, which brought the number of people in the homestead of Yves Albatrois, maker of guitars, to around forty, and there were a few more visitors to arrive, within the next couple of hours.

The afternoon had cooled a few degrees, and it was noticeable. The males, who numbered around fifteen, were outside at the table and also at the inside table, in the kitchen; in a half an hour the chromatic evening would expand into prevalence and the gravel outside the house would find patrons of the children of the visitors and not the males, who were walking around, outside of the homestead, through the plantations, which were not far from the homestead and the main building. The males were to find themselves in the basement, with the casks of wine and with the apertures. The music was to begin, and the fricative and mannish drink had not feigned, in any of its consumers, not Pantagathus nor Tavis, the heretic; not Yves Albatrois, maker of guitars; and in neither Mpoulo nor Moz, all of whom were to descend into the basement, with their respective instrumentation, Tavis, the heretic, and Yves Albatrois, maker of guitars, with their guitars, and Mpoulo and Moz, with their clarinos, except Pantagathus, who was to watch and listen, and all musicians were to perform for the visitors and for the festivities, and for all, who decided to find themselves in the basement, with the apse and with the preternatural alms.

The guitars were in hand. The clarinos were in hand, too. The chairs had been placed in an area in between the casks of wine, and the musicians were facing the apertures and the corner of the basement, which conjoined the two walls, bordered by the outdoors. The wine had been drinked and fifteen people were in the basement, with the musicians and with the vas; the guitars had been struck, in the chords and in their crackled tricks. The clarinos were the jest. Pantagathus was inflatable, by the clarinos. They resided in his loins, the wooden notes buoyant in his abdomen, which was hysterical, and which was daffy.

Tavis, the heretic, was doing what Yves Albatrois, maker of guitars, had mentioned earlier, regarding the key of C, and Tavis, the heretic, was in the key of A, in the slippery key of C's stead. The quatuor had rehearsed, it did occur to Pantagathus and the listeners. The song, which was being played, was a cohesive stretch of notes and harmonics—the musicians, Tavis, the heretic, Yves Albatrois, maker of guitars, and the clarino players, Mpoulo and Moz, were blinded by the awareness, which came with musicality; they were nothing; they were not people; they were not musicians; they were contiguous and one—and Tavis, the heretic, had arisen in his key and the music did splatter into the ninth, and then Tavis, the heretic, hit twice a note and Pantagathus saw lights where there were none, the song having ended and Tavis, the heretic, saying, "I need to take you home, because I need chocolate," and the subsequent song began, with the clarinos and with the conversation, which was taking place in between the listeners, because the song was quiet, and which was taking place in between the clarinos, because they were senescent; Tavis, the heretic, said, in the ill lit basement, what he had intuited, in regards to the scenario, which was in place in the hills of Kosmidion, and which was in contiguity, southwards, in the city of Constantinople, "It looks like a chocolate cake," because he had taken eight drinks of the mannish drink, and because it was severe, the clarinos, dabbed into one another, the guitars, sprinkled into the song, with the succulence and with the cloister. The song ended, and Tavis, the heretic, said, "I can tell a better story than that," the clarinos hit, and Tavis, the heretic, "I'm a conceited fogging idiot. I'm so conceited," and it was then the conversation of the festivities took a step towards abandon, the haggard, which were considerable.

2017

In New York City, during the week of Thanksgiving, which was Thanksgiving in New York City, and not in Newfoundland and Labrador—the family of Pete Tsiminis liked the holiday was ensuing, and had decided also to partake in the Thanksgiving and New Yorker traditions— Pete Tsiminis found himself in Central Park. He and his parents were walking through the park, and it was dry. It was cold, and not too cold to enjoy the Central Park grandiose, with the rocks and with the walks.

The grasses were not of the summer or springtime Central Park viridian. They had dried out and only a little bit; their color was of a dehydrated viridian, and it was close to Hunyadi yellow, with the dryness and with the appropriate wet. It was granular when Pete Tsiminis had lain on the grasses. They were supple. It was Thanksgiving. New York City was agreeable, in that stretch of time, which was a week in length, and which was ephemeral. On Monday, people were regular. There was a particular whip in the Central Park grandiose, in that stretch. It was not unpleasant. People went to Central Park for the whip, and it was a whip of fabric against the lips; it was of importance, in the stretch, in which Pete Tsiminis had lain on the Central

Park grasses, and it was a pugnacious whip. It made Pete Tsiminis have pity. There was pity for the grasses. Of course, there was pity for the grasses. Pete Tsiminis had pity for the Thanksgiving week, and also he had pity for the people, who celebrated Thanksgiving. He had pity for New York City. He had pity for the lunch, which was scheduled to occur, following the walk through Central Park; he had pity for Central Park. It was Thanksgiving. He had pity for the beets he had seen, at the market further downtown. He had pity for the poet in the streets.

He did decide to lie in the grasses and get pity. It would be over fast. It would be as if pity had never happened. Pete Tsiminis had had breakfast in the morning. Of course, he had had breakfast in the morning. It was New York City. It was Thanksgiving. He remarked to his father, "She still hasn't eaten her muffin." There were two muffins. Both were cinnamon and pumpkin muffins. "The muffins are getting old and the coffee is getting cold." Pete Tsiminis had said the remarks to his father, who was sitting beside the mother of Pete Tsiminis. The mother of Pete Tsiminis was silent, and she looked disconcerted. It was Thanksgiving. If there were a reason to be disconcerted during Thanksgiving, it was Thanksgiving. Pete Tsiminis had lain in the grasses of Central Park, two hours following breakfast. He had been lying in the grass for ten minutes. It was cold and tolerable. The parents of Pete Tsiminis were sitting at a bench, along one of the walks, close by where Pete Tsiminis had lain, in referentiality. The grasses had suggested he lie left lateral decubitus. He had not taken them up, in their suggestibility. The clear Central Park troposphere suggested Pete Tsiminis bum in the sticks. Pete Tsiminis had not taken up the tropospheric Central Park, either, in their suggestibility. The rock, which was high, and which was large and demarcated, suggested Pete Tsiminis come touch the cold igneous. Pete Tsiminis did not go and touch the cold Central Park rocks. Also, the goldeneye ducks suggested he watch and whistle. Pete Tsiminis did not go towards the goldeneye duck, and he did not watch, nor did he whistle. Instead, Pete Tsiminis had lain in the grasses of Central Park and had stayed lain, for five minutes, and then there was pity and taste. He was to approach his parents, who were sitting at a bench, alongside the walk nearest the grasses, on which Pete Tsiminis had lain, and they would go to lunch at a delicatessen his mother suggested they visit, because it was the only day in the year, outside of Halloween, they gave you a slice of pumpkin cake. It was Thanksgiving and it was New York City. The mother of Pete Tsiminis was to have it no other way than that, in the pugnacious whip and in the turkey lunch, which was the matter. They gave to the gaiety.

They walked a little bit uptown. They decided to get a cab, because it was a little further north than was comfortable to walk, that is the delicatessen was a little further northwards, and Pete Tsiminis and his parents had no problem getting a cab. It was New York City. People got cabs. People got turkey sandwiches. People got pity and garrulous. The small delicatessen was small and smaller than the mother of Pete Tsiminis preconceived. The small area was thirty square feet. It was allotted with four tables and a small bar, at which three people were eating sandwiches. One person was at the bar and he was not eating a sandwich.

He was eating his pumpkin cake. "Yum." The mother of Pete Tsiminis was situated on the inside of the table. Beside her was the father of Pete Tsiminis. They were facing the bar, over which was a blackboard. On the blackboard was a turkey, drawn with chalk. The turkey was well drawn. It had much plumage. Pete Tsiminis was on the outside of the table and was facing the wall, which was charcoal gray, and Pete Tsiminis was out of his jacket, which had made him warm fast, in the delicatessen. The kitchen was visible through a small window, further past the bar, which was on the left-hand side, upon entrance. The kitchen was for roast beef, pastrami, ham, and bacon, if somebody wanted a roast beef sandwich or a pastrami sandwich or a ham or bacon sandwich, with a preheat. None of the three, Pete Tsiminis nor his parents, were to get the roast beef sandwich, nor the pastrami sandwich, and they were not to get the ham or bacon sandwich. They were to get the turkey sandwich, because it was Thanksgiving. The parade was further centric, in the island. They decided to forgo the parade. It was calamitous. For the turkey and for the Thanksgiving sake, they stayed away from the parade and hit Central Park in the parade's stead, following which they went to get a turkey sandwich, at the delicatessen. The sandwich, by three, was taken to their table. The father of Pete Tsiminis was drinking a whiskey. The delicatessen was a bar, which sold liquor. It was not a typical bar one were to visit upon drinking in the evenings. The delicatessen did serve liquor and for purposes much inclined towards the agreeability of the father of Pete Tsiminis, and the father of Pete Tsiminis was agreeable to great effects.

The turkey sandwich had been cut into two triangles. There was the turkey sandwich on the right-hand side of the plate. On the left-hand side of the plate, there was chips. Pete Tsiminis repositioned his turkey sandwich. He put one triangle in the top left of the plate and he put the other triangle in the top right of the plate, with the hypotenuses downwards, and in the middle of the plate, he put his chips, for symmetry. Toothpicks were in the triangles. He removed one toothpick and began to eat the triangle, with the hypotenuse first. He was a young person. He ate the hypotenuse first. That was what young people did in New York City, on Thanksgiving, and then the recapitulation would arise. The cab ride was the stretch, during which Pete Tsiminis saw what he needed to do, following the delicatessen. It was a small record joint. It was called The Record Joint. Pete Tsiminis did not want anything from The Record Joint. He only wanted to stop into The Record Joint and check out the poster of Elton John, which was a life size poster of Elton John, with his glasses and with his diastema. Elton John and his disposition did not change. It was a poster and it was life size. The actual disposition of Elton John might have changed, for all Pete Tsiminis knew. He would have to ask him. That kind of baby happened in New York City. The sign on the front of The Record Joint read Five for Four. Pete Tsiminis was into his second triangle of turkey sandwich. It was in the latter triangle of turkey sandwich when Pete Tsiminis regarded The Record Joint. He mused, They give you four. They give you five. He finished his sandwich. The window had been open in the cab ride. It was not warm, nor was it hot, as New York City tended to be, in the summer and springtime Central Park viridian. One were to open the window and leave the window open and it is not like the monkey breath, mused the father of Pete Tsiminis. It had been in the stretch with The Record Joint and the life size poster of Elton John, with his glasses and with his diastema when the father of Pete Tsiminis made the derivation. The three had finished their turkey sandwiches and the waitress brought over the slice of pumpkin cake. Also, she brought over three forks. They ate the slice of pumpkin cake, and then they were outside and back into the Thanksgiving afternoon, which was peaking at an incredulous thirty-nine degrees Fahrenheit. Pete Tsiminis hit them with the suggestion, "Let's go to The Record Joint."

The mother of Pete Tsiminis said, "What is The Record Joint?"

"I saw The Record Joint further downtown. It's a joint that sells records. What else would it be? It's The Record Joint."

"Let's go to The Record Joint," said the father of Pete Tsiminis, and Pete Tsiminis took them towards The Record Joint, and not at all in extemporaneity. Pete Tsiminis was walking down the street, with the cabs and with the pedestrians. There was a constriction in his thoracic cavity. It was not demanding. It was subtle. The constriction was present and Pete Tsiminis regarded the deposit, which was not of fixity. It moved and, of its own accord, regarded different shops and storefronts, and it regarded people and cars and acoustics. It was not at all of fixity.

Pete Tsiminis walked through pocket after pocket of constriction. First, it was the shop beside the delicatessen, where they had their turkey sandwich. The shop beside the delicatessen was a souvenir shop. It sold postcards on rotating towers. It sold baseball caps and T-shirts. It sold coffee cups and tumblers. Also, it sold lighters of the Zippo kind and it sold trinkets along the lines of stickers and necklaces. It was in front of the souvenir shop when Pete Tsiminis first noticed the constriction, and then Pete Tsiminis found himself outside of the shop, which was further down the street, and which sold T-shirts and shoes, of its own line. The constriction had receded, once past the souvenir shop, and then it had become again manifest, in front of the fashion store. It, too, went away; Pete Tsiminis hit the grocery and the pretzel stand, both of which received him with the constriction. Pocket after pocket, Pete Tsiminis found himself in the constrictions.

They were concave and convex pockets of constrictions. The received him and expelled him, in subsequence, and there was no seemliness about the exchange. It was an immaterial exchange. It accepted Pete Tsiminis into the concavity and Pete Tsiminis was bowed into a curve, and then he was reformed afterwards. The convex pockets assumed the form of Pete Tsiminis, who, in the two seconds during which the convexity and he were together, had assumed a spherical person. There were pockets of constriction. There were concave and convex pockets.

The Record Joint was of importance. Pete Tsiminis found The Record Joint with ease. In he walked, and the parents were behind him, and they, the three of them, smelled the wooden and plastic smell of the The Record Joint, which had a tune on the speakers, and the song had just begun: "When I'm old and losing my hair, many years from now—" An employee approached Pete Tsiminis. She said, "Can I help you find anything? Are you looking for a peculiar artist? Is he American?"

"No, thanks," Pete Tsiminis said. "I'm looking around."

"Of course. I'm over here." She went back to her counter and continued with some scanning of records. There were records and compact disks, in The Record Joint. Pete Tsiminis was not interested in them. Rather, he had looked at the Elton John life size poster, which was outside and shown through the glass window, with his glasses and with his diastema; and then, he went inside and found himself talking to the employee, who was wearing a T-shirt, on which was printed Schwarz Fräulein, and Pete Tsiminis got an eye full of Axle Rose, who, too was a life size poster, on the wall of The Record Joint, with his denim and with his teeth. They did not stay long in The Record Joint. They were in and soon they were back out in the streets, searching for a shop, which sold suitcases.

There was gravitation. The constriction was bygone. The pockets of concave and convex constriction were gone, and gravitation had taken its place, in the form of footfalls— footfall after footfall after footfall. The mother of Pete Tsiminis had said, "I'm going to want another bag. I left the room over at the hotel, so I could get some cool air, and I decided I didn't need another bag. We have fifteen minutes before we hit the U.S.S. Intrepid. I want another bag."

The father of Pete Tsiminis said, "Let's get another bag," and the gravitation had occurred to Pete Tsiminis, who was placing footfall after footfall after footfall, all the same footfall, the same footfalls of Pete Tsiminis, with the same feet, walking in the same place, at high noon, walking with the metalloids and with the fortuity.

There was a footstep, which lead the person of Pete Tsiminis, and it was the left footstep; and there was, in subsequence, a footstep, which supported the person of Pete Tsiminis, and it was the right footstep. Footstep after footstep, it was the leading left and the supporting right. The weight of Pete Tsiminis was distributed, with equanimity. The left foot fell, and then the right foot fell, and the left foot was of lead and the right foot was of tin, and the grandiose was that of the hysteria to walk on water. There was no quadrupedal distribution. There was no diagonal spatiality, as there was in the Canis lupus familiaris. It was Pete Tsiminis. He was not a quadruped. No quadruped was to be named Pete Tsiminis. His feet were of the anthropoid, and they were distributed, in terms of the gravitation, with their bipedal grandiose. There were two feet, not four feet— the lead and leading footsteps and the tin and supporting footsteps made pasty ways towards that which was the same place, walking with the hæmoid and with the flibbertygibbity, towards graham crackers and towards Basalt Road—Cletus of importance, and Cletus, with his meek adieu, following which Pete Tsiminis went into his house, to change and to have a glass of water upstairs, with his poster from the Museum of Modern Art and his metallic apple and the brass spoon from an antiquity dealer, which the parents of Pete Tsiminis had wanted to visit, while in New York City, in the weekend of Thanksgiving and of the Elton John life size poster, with his glasses and with his diastema. The footfalls had brought him to the location they had brought him, and Pete Tsiminis was exasperated from the walk through the snow, past the hill, which had been moddled, and past the Coleman's, where he and Jonathon had bought the large marshmallows and the cinnamon graham crackers.

Jonathon had not been to school since the breakage of his ankle. Pete Tsiminis was making a schedule in mind, the one week of healing and rest for Jonathon and his foot, and made the following Monday the day he was to return to school, and then noticed the winter break was to occur in the subsequent week, which meant Jonathon might not go back to school and Pete Tsiminis and his footfalls were to gravitate, in their leaden and tin composite and in lonesomeness, one after another, footfall after footfall after footfall—they are meant to mutilate, the spill of the profane and the six articles of clothing, removed and replaced, for Pete Tsiminis to well know, and with fullness and with immunity, that he had changed and had gone to the house of Jonathon to rail his nuts.

2017

The Betulaceæ woods were to have a visitor. Pete Tsiminis had decided to enter, and he had a peculiar objective. His parents did not like him going into the Betulaceæ woods when it had been snowing, and when there was snow on the ground of the Betulaceæ woods. To go out into Betulaceæ woods for a short amount of time was all right, even with the snow on the ground of the Betulaceæ woods and with the temperature at three degrees Centigrade. Pete Tsiminis was going into the Betulaceæ woods for about an hour. He did have a peculiar objective, and it was to be completed within an hour, the travels to the point at which the interest was located and the return trip to the house on Basalt Road, included; he had been naughty.

The clothes, articles of all types and sizes, were put onto his person. The long johns and the T-shirt were put onto the person of Pete Tsiminis. The snow pants and sweatshirt were assumed; and the snow jacket was put onto his person, as were the gloves, socks, and boots—all of which was put onto the person of Pete Tsiminis, in systematic intention—before which, Pete Tsiminis made a lunch and filled a thermos with the tea his mother had gotten from the apothecary.

He did not bring his pipe. The Betulaceæ woods were not going to have a Pete Tsiminis, in mid smoke, though he did live by the aphorism, Whittle your pipes, which was his aphorism until he realized he was a jest. He was prepared. His person was covered with snow time effects. His lunch was in his backpack, and his thermos, with the tea his mother had gotten from the apothecary, was slung around his shoulder, with instantaneity.

A minute of deliberation had become thirty seconds of urination, and then Pete Tsiminis was quite in candor, with the snow effects and with the sustenance. The minute of deliberation, following which were the thirty seconds of urination, was the hike in its preconception, and Pete Tsiminis was to be hiking, an hour in total, a half an hour to the interest and a half an hour in return. All of the segmentated movements were the œconomical progeny of five hundred thousand specimen Betulaceæ in Newfoundland and Labrador, and all the microbials were infinity, within which were many an infinity, and Pete Tsiminis was naughty, because he was to be in the Betulaceæ for one hour, which may well have been, in those five hundred thousand specimen Betulaceæ, infinity, within which were many an infinity. There was the Pete Tsiminis, the mighty. It was not Pete Tsiminis, the mighty. It was Pete Tsiminis, of mircotonality. It was Pete Tsiminis, with his footfalls, one after the other, footfall after footfall after footfall, with the leaden left and the tin right, and all in one place, with the same feet and with same the couple of footfalls, Pete Tsiminis, not the mighty, not of microtonality; it was Pete Tsiminis, of microseismicity.

It was the Pete Tsiminis, of kinetomechanisticality, who was to traverse eastwards, towards the point of interest. As long as Pete Tsiminis was not Joe Pesci, it was all right, because Pete Tsiminis was in the Betulaceæ wood and he was going to be in the Betulaceæ wood for an hour, and then Pete Tsiminis was to make it back to the house on Basalt Road, in good posture. He was always a person of good posture. He had never had bad posture. Pete Tsiminis passed the place, where Jonathon had sat, with his broken ankle, against the Betulaceæ. He had met Jonathon in the fourth grade. It was an exchange, which was a surprise, and which was the initiation of a friendship. The family of Jonathon had moved into the house on Basalt Road, and Pete Tsiminis had come outside and found Jonathon lying in the grasses, and Pete Tsiminis sprinkled grass on Jonathon. What was I thinking? Pete Tsiminis and his posture mused, walking through the Betulaceæ. Afterwards, Pete Tsiminis took Jonathon in the Tsiminis house for pastry.

Two years later, Pete Tsiminis was composing a menu. There was asparagus incorporated. Jonathon was to come over, with the ankle and with the raillery. They were to have asparagus. The hike through the Betulaceæ was at hand. The asparagus came afterwards. It was the hike, through the Betulaceæ, and the dinner, which was the matter, made only water only water. It was the hike, through the Betulaceæ, and the dinner, which made the ground a resource of inquiry—Does this look like a place one can drink only water?—and Pete Tsiminis stopped his hike, for only seconds. He took a drink of the tea his mother had gotten from the apothecary.

A quadruped, a specimen Cervidæ—This guy feels I'm on deck—was seen, and the deer jumped through a pair of Betulaceæ. Pete Tsiminis would have to call in thunder and take this home. He was jest. The Cervidæ was long gone. In the top drawer of the nightstand of Pete Tsiminis, with the brass spoon, there were a couple of disposable cameras. The Betulaceæ belonged in the reel of pictures. It was spurious, in its infinity, and once more Pete Tsiminis was thinking of numbers.

The Betulaceæ was traversed, slow, and Pete Tsiminis was the technician of the half cent. Pete Tsiminis was the cut; he was wanton. The tea was drinked, once more, and Pete Tsiminis did clean off his lips, with his tongue; he had gotten bigger. There was a layer of fat all around. It was not unpleasant. The aphorism by which Pete Tsiminis had lived, Whittle your pipes, had been assumed by Jonathon, who was rather nascent, in the commencement of the sixth grade, and the aphorism became deux, that is, Tweak your tits, Throw your shoulders, because he, too, was a killer.

Pete Tsiminis looked behind him and saw his footprints. Pete Tsiminis and Jonathon had gotten into only one fight, and even then, it was not a fight of physicality. Jonathon had clapped Pete Tsiminis hard on the back, and Pete Tsiminis told him if he were to hit him on the back again, he was to tweak his tits and throw his shoulders.

Jonathon did reply, "Are you making threats?" The rhotic consonant had been hit. "Are you making threats?" If Jonathon were a power tool, he would be the jackhammer. That was what it said, "Are you making threats?"

Pete Tsiminis said, "Not even close."

Pete Tsiminis put his hindfoot in the Betulaceæ wood floor, with the heel and with the ankle. The foot rolled onto the midfoot, and the pyramid arch took place; and then, the forefoot gained perspective, with its five phalanges. Jonathon and his rhotic consonant, "Are you making threats?" wound Pete Tsiminis into the hollow of a thicket—Will it close its mouth?—and the coal of the igneous rocks and also the water, which was just audible, and the glass, which differentiated the inside of the house on Basalt Road and the specimens Betulaceæ was relevant to Pete Tsiminis, because the Betulaceæ had become a mine field and the laundry wanted extra clothing in its lot, this evening; the hike was relevant and Pete Tsiminis, at that point in the hike, did like anybody, because they were cushions against the fatigue. Pete Tsiminis stopped and drinked tea, before which he had tasted the salt on his lips.

1453

The mannish drink had taken its duration. The indium of morning was coming into the basement, where Pantagathus and Tavis, the heretic, Yves Albatrois, maker of guitars, Mpoulo and Moz, were resided, with a few other people and with the music. The music had not stopped, in entirety. In the stretches, during which it did stop, the music stopped for only ten minutes or thirty minutes at most—Tavis, the heretic, getting wine, or Yves Albatrois, maker of guitars, getting bread, or Mpoulo or Moz going outside, through the cellar door and into the high morning of Kosmidion to malnutriate—and then, the music was commenced and people were to dance and make jocular staccato, in the midst of the music and of the nullity.

The mannish drink had taken its duration, and the effects had become of a soporific and a stimulant to Pantagathus, who was going upstairs, through the senescent staircase, which was not unpleasant, and up through the staircase, which brought him to the second floor of the homestead of Yves Albatrois, maker of guitars, and then further upwards, in the staircase on the opposite end of the second floor and onto the third floor and his bedroom, with the embroidery.

Pantagathus had lain down, and he was taken by Constantinople. The harlots had taken Constantinople, and there was trouble still in the city, though the people were most expired, and though the city was demarcated to extreme extents—the fires of the burning villages, which surrounded the city of Constantinople; the explosions of the cannon fire, which had made the city walls of no affectation; the metallic strikes of metal on marble, in the walls of the Hagia Sophia—and Pantagathus thinking, Everybody is murdering each other. There was a bookcase to the right-hand side of the bed of Pantagathus, and it was illuminated by the high indium coming in from the window, which was drawn in its blinds. There were few books. Pantagathus glanced at them and noticed they were of the philosophia of the age of the new Constantinople, in regards to the religion of the city, which was Orthodox, and which was Orthodox no longer, and also there were history books, of which the period of time in question was the 1099 People's Crusades, which started the ceaseless war in between the eastern peoples, Byzantion, and the Romans, and there were books, which took the historiography of the crusades all the way to the Albigensian Crusade, in Iberia, and the Children's Crusade—My books are here, the priest Pantagathus mused—and he had arisen from his bed and opened the window. It was warm, and there was not much difference in the temperature, after it was opened. The shirt of Pantagathus had assumed a heaviness, and he did decide to get it off his body, because it was in the month of August, and because it did not require much humility to do that which was warranted, to take off the shirt and to take off the pants, and then lie in bed and sleep for hours, in the ascending morning and with the intemperate climax.

There were no socks, with which Pantagathus had to work. He had his shoes and his socks outside, around the side of the homestead of Yves Albatrois, maker of guitars, because there had been a little bit of wet, which had descended upon the shoes and socks, and they were to be in the sun to dry.

The third floor was comfortable and hot. Pantagathus was asleep, and he had lain down with the intention of sleeping until noon, when the homestead of Yves Albatrois, maker of guitars, was to once again take life. The eyes of Pantagathus had seen the refined watches of the genteel, and the watches were on the wrists, and they were making their elliptical circuitry, in the long hand, with the wheels and with the quartz. The eyes of Pantagathus retained the discombobulations, which had arrived him in sleep. There were inventions and many of which Pantagathus could not place—there were the watches, on the wrists of the genteel, with the long hand and with the quartz; and there were telescopic devices; and there were miniature cannons; and there were solutions, which were made to cure ailments— and many of these inventions were met with an individual, or a notion, which was the creator, or progenitor of the respective creations, and Pantagathus retained many of the individuals and their intentions, too, upon waking in the tawdry climax. It is his choices, which are the problem, Pantagathus musing on the creator, or progenitor of the telescopic device; and this is his problem, regarding the maker of the miniature cannon; and we do not want anything to do with him, in reference to the solutions, made to cure the ailments.

Matter of fact, the reticence of the inventions, in Pantagathus, brought him back to sleep, and the priest, sleeping, did hear somebody come into his room, and then the person had left the room, and Pantagathus was quite exhaustible, from the festivities and from the inventions, and so much so that he did not need to retain the inventions any more than he who was to invent the inventions needed to invent inventions, because the inventors were separate from their inventions, and because exhaustion was separate from any festivity—He is separate, mused Pantagathus, and that was all regarding the inventions and their inventors; he got hit with the brilliance and decided to break expectations. He decided to have you break yourself, and Pantagathus did forget something in regards to the mother, who was abound, and who was covering the homestead of Yves Albatrois, maker of guitars, with heat and with suggestions.

Pantagathus put his feet on the floor. He arose and went into the hallway to investigate the person, who had come into his bedroom, and who had left—Nobody's there—and Pantagathus went down the stairs and onto the second floor and further downwards, towards the first floor and towards his shoes and socks.

He was dressed in his clothes, once more, and he did not speak to anybody. There were few people awake. Most were still asleep. He found his shoes and socks where he had put them the night prior, and he took them and went to the kitchen, where there was water, and were there were a few rags.

There was wine all over the socks. It was as if somebody had nailed his feet. There was no cleaning the socks of the wine, in entirety; Pantagathus brought the shoes and socks back upstairs to his bedroom, on the third floor. He went into his room and put down the socks and shoes on the floor, and decided to flip this linen into halves and to rest his feet on the linens, which were then at the foot of his bed; Pantagathus picked a book from the bookshelf. It was the Albigensian Crusades. He opened the book and a picture of Barbara came out of the cover and onto his chest. He read a little bit of the Albigensian Crusades. There were people downstairs, and they were moving and talking loud. Pantagathus heard, "Where is the cheese?" and then he heard the sounds of the clarino. It was Mpoulo playing the clarino, Pantagathus gathered, because it was the same decrescendo Mpoulo had discovered the first night of the festivities. Pantagathus did remark on the decrescendo the first night of the festivities. "You are going to be popular, play like that," he had said; and then, the morning following, when Pantagathus was reading the Albigensian Crusades, he heard a small difference in the decrescendo, for which Mpoulo had been searching the night prior, and mused, This guy is famous. Mpoulo hit a slew of notes. He's everywhere. There was an explosion far away, in the distance, and Pantagathus ignored it. There were a few more explosions, which followed the original explosion, and Pantagathus regarded, in a slight wince of his lip, the explosions and their demolitions people, with their lexical advancement and with their feet; he then once more ignored the barrage, as much as he was able, and donned it mere interjection and other isolate.

1923

Panagiotis and the old man were sitting in the capital L courtyard. They had been discussing a topic, which had been of interest to Panagiotis for some weeks. Their residence in the homestead, in Kassitera, had been four weeks in total. All, who had taken up residence in Kassitera, and who had traversed through Eptadendros, were contented with the homestead, in Kassitera, with the drink and with the children, all except Panagiotis, who had been having an idea oscillate in his head for the latter two weeks of his residence, in Kassitera, and which incorporated four items—wheat, hop pellets, yeast, and sugar. The idea had been suggested to the old man in the third week of residence, and the old man suggested they converse on the topic in some day, in the beginning of the fourth week, which was the matter, and which was then in its very early hours, on 18 Sunday 1923; the topic in question was the inclusion of malt wheat beer, in the distillery shed, closer the corral. "We would need to imbibe the ingredients for ninety or one-hundred and twenty minutes, and then the malt wheat would be near complete. It is simple and worthy. Have you had wheat beer? I have had it in Constantinople, many times."

"I have not had wheat beer. Constantinople has many privileges. We do not have the wheat beer, here in Kassitera," said the old man. "That may well change."

"Why not? It is worthy and tasteful, with cheese."

"I do think you are correct in that," said the old man.

"Let us malt the beer. It will be of no labor on your part."

"Why not? Malt the beer, and allow me to taste the first of the malt beer with you and your compatriots."

"It will be done, Kireio. The question, which dawns on me now is the time at which to malt the beer. It is not the hot season. It is getting cooler, but I do not foresee that as a problem. Besides—" Panagiotis had been interrupted by a young niece. She was frantic and hysterical.

"Papou, Zuny is having her babies. Come, too, Panagiotis. Zuny is having her babies and it sounds like the demon."

"Don't say that, Anna," said the old man.

"Come, Papou. Come, Panagiotis. Zuny is having her babies. I will get Aristo."

"Come," said the old man. "Let us see Zuny, who is having her babies." The old man had arisen, and Panagiotis went with him to the corral, where the pups were heard, and many people were in the shed, within which Zuny had lain for some days, Harito being one of them, and also Santeia was in the shed, with Zuny, the niece and nephew Anna and Aristo, and two other adults and two other children, whom Panagiotis did not recognize, were in the shed, and Zuny was having her babies, with the amniotic fluid and with the teeth.

They removed themselves from the shed, afterwards, and the two adults and the two children, whom Panagiotis did not recognize went northwards, and Harito and Sanetia,

Panagiotis and the old man, went towards the homestead. Santeia and the old man went to sit down in the capital L courtyard. Panagiotis and Harito went to laboratory, around the side of the homestead, and Harito began to juggle the children. Panagiotis finished his wine skin, and went to the shed, where Stefangianopoulou was working on the invention, and it showed little progress, as far is Panagiotis could see. It was in its forthright position, standing on four legs, and the thresh was connected to a spout, which were the only two differences Panagiotis had noticed since his first visit to the shed of Stefangianopoulou and his invention; and then, he went back to the laboratory, where Harito was juggling children. Harito had put down the children and approached Panagiotis, and they refilled the wine skin, with the casks, below the homestead.

"Let us give wine to Zuny," said Panagiotis.

"It may be too late to have any good effect."

"Let us take wine to the dogs, and if Zuny does not have wine Zito will, I can assure you." Panagiotis and Harito went to the corral and poured wine in the bowl of Zuny and Zito. The placenta and the amniotic fluid had been consumed. It was an exchange unparalleled. In the shed, Harito got close to the pups. Zito did bar his teeth. "Were we not supposed to take wine to the bitch?" said Panagiotis, upon leaving the corral. Zito did have his emotionality, and that had come with the wine and with the cacophony. At the capital L courtyard, dry meats had been placed on the table. The plantation workers had come in for a lunch.

1453

The Helios had arched into full Shemesh. The priest, Pantagathus, had went to sleep at six o'clock A.M., and he had seen the indium come from the topography of Kosmidion; and then, he had awoken to the discombobulations of the watches and miniature cannons and the other inventions. He had the notion somebody had come into his room, investigated to find nobody was there, and then went downstairs and retrieved his socks and shoes, which were against the wall of the bedroom, where he resided then, when the Helios made full arch, and when it was full Shemesh, the cicadas in colloquy and the manariza in the apprehension of energy.

The Albigensian Crusades had been glanced upon and the picture of Barbara had been replaced in the inside of the *Algibensian Crusades*, which belonged on the bookshelf, where it resided in that bedroom, with the shocked noon and with the wheat. Pantagathus looked outside of the window, which he had opened. Many people were visible in the plantation. Nobody was working. The fig trees were systematic in their placement, and people were huddled closer the main building; they were discussing something, which was audible to Pantagathus, but which was indecipherable at the height, three floors upwards. Fifteen people were visible in the back of the homestead of Yves Albatrois, maker of guitars, and upon descending the staircases, Pantagathus found about ten or twelve more throughout the homestead, in the kitchen and in the basement, which still had its apertures open, and which was the most comfortable room in the homestead and just as well all of Kosmidion—Tavis, the heretic, and Yves Albatrois, maker of guitars, were two of those in the basement, and they were sitting on the wicker chairs they had been the night prior. All exchanged formalities, and Pantagathus went outside, in the back of the house, with the fifteen people, who, he learned, were discussing going out into the figs.

The figs were not far away; it was a fifty pace walk and the fig trees began. One could see the fig trees from the place, where the discussion was being held, close by the homestead and under the window of the bedroom of Pantagathus. They did stride towards the figs. Pantagathus had eaten nothing in the morning time, and neither had the people, who had been discussing entering the figs and having a breakfast, and with whom Pantagathus had become well acquainted, over the wine of the first night of the festivities, and with the music and with the vas. They were to breakfast in the figs, and people were strewn throughout the figs, eating the fruit and flirting with one another, and the children were throwing figs at one another at one point, to which one of the adults did shout for them to stop, because the fruits were food and how much longer could they withstand their own capital? The children were throwing figs for only thirty seconds longer, and then they ceased their raucousness. Pantagathus took a fig and peeled it; he was with a girl, with whom he had become rather more so than acquainted, but even with whom he had become philistine. They did not talk much. They ate figs and she said, "I slept in the figs after the wine," to which Pantagathus said they all should have slept in the figs; the figs were a milieu of wanton and aromatics. They all should have slept in the figs.

Tavis, the heretic, had approached the figs. He regarded the girl, with weightlessness, and said, "Bread is inside." He said to come inside of the homestead, because there was bread, and not to tell anybody.

2017

The Betulaceæ went on for a long while; kilometer after kilometer the Betulaceæ ranged onwards, until it hit the maple wood, at which point the Betulaceæ became the maple; Pete Tsiminis was not going that far into the wood, nor did he have any intention of going that far into the wood. His peculiar objective was not to take him to the maple; it was closer the house of the Tsiminis where the peculiar objective and the point of interest were located. Pete Tsiminis had been walking through the Betulaceæ for twenty minutes, and the point of interest was up ahead—a glimpse into the ravine, which was some one hundred meters downwards, and in which resided all kinds of sub-aquatic fauna, from trout to oysters, in their incongruous habitat. The fish, which resided in the ravine, were caught with rarity. In the stretch of ravine, for which Pete Tsiminis was hunting, the fossiliferous stratum went straight up on either side of the ravine, and the waters were fast and loud. The ravine, in the stretch, for which Pete Tsiminis was hunting, was narrow and it was perilous, in the area towards which Pete Tsiminis was walking. The parents of Pete Tsiminis did know of the area in the Betulaceæ, where the gradient did undulate downwards, and then, from its ease in topographics, become a stark downhill, at the end of which, the fossiliferous stratum did assume its innate aggresivity. The gradient was shallow, and five meters outwards, the downhill undulation picked up, and the ravine was visible through a thicket of Betulaceæ, with the clarity and with the phonics.

The other side of the ravine was, too, visible. Pete Tsiminis had seen the gap in the Betulaceæ once, and he had seen the ravine and the opposite side of the ravine, and he had been apprehensive; the loudness and the arterial stratum, as well as the seeming adolescence in Pete Tsiminis, had made him apprehensive; he had relinquished his apprehensiveness, in most scenarios, as of the recent two years, when the reality of middle school was prevalent, and when he had begun to enjoy isolation, in the Betulaceæ and otherwise in any area, where the nonsense of children and the cacophony of Newfoundland and Labrador were of hesitancy. In the in between segments of jests, Newfoundland and Labrador did extend a residency towards Pete Tsiminis, in the form of the incisiveness and in the form of the occasional twig snapping under the weight of the Cervidæ, or just as well his own; and also in the form of the ravine, for which Pete Tsiminis was hunting, and which was never too far from mind. One looked across the ravine and saw the opposite end of the fossiliferous stratum, which had been eroded over millennia, in Newfoundland and Labrador, by the ravine, with its incomplete spherics and with the bones of Mammalia placed throughout the stratum, as if by a systematic hand, which had also made the fossils of the Precambrian, in its seemliness, and also the Batrachians.

The sulfuric pits had construed themselves as volcanic mountains. The deterioration of the area was evident, and it did reconstrue itself into the paradisiac locale that was Newfoundland and Labrador; the deterioration had taken place, and then there was the surfaced hydrate and the descended pressurization, which met on the crust, and which were apt to make an incubator for the deciduous trees, through which Pete Tsiminis was walking, and also the Cervidæ and the ravine, in its perpetual movement and destructivity.

The tectonic plates had shifted and it was unnoticeable; the evidence created misconceptions, and there were not only misconceptions. There were misconceptions within misconceptions, and they all were interlaced and of affectation. It was the ecology—the igneous rock and the metamorphic rock, the fauna and flora, the lichen and senescent philosophy—which made footfalls footfalls. It made no speech. It did not talk.

1923

Panagiotis had started his preparation for the distillery addition. It was a preparation of motivation and not a preparation of materials, wood, glass jars, and a metal barrel. That came later, when Panagiotis had tricked himself into motivation. He had been following the plantation workers out towards the potatoes. The plantation workers' party was tonight, and a harvest was made, small as it was, and Panagiotis had accompanied the plantation workers, of which there were two, a girl, named Tina and her sister, to the potato field, for an appropriate sized harvest. They had made it to the potato farm, and Tina had made a remark, something regarding a wheat loaf and two potatoes coming together for a particular bake; and Panagiotis said, "Stefangianoulou can do it. He's been up to everything in this place."

"—and then it would be a mixture of the two."

"—He does everything in this place. He doesn't even know what he's doing. Nobody knows what he's doing."

"Get some potatoes."

Panagiotis took three potatoes. The girls quite filled their dresses with potatoes. "Where did you get such knowledge of cuisine?"

"I got it from my mother. It came by itself. I picked it up. What am I going to do?"

"Bake some wheat loaf potato bread."

"It just comes naturally to me."

"You must pick up things well."

It had been an exchange. Tina was an inquisitive girl. Nobody paid much attention to her. Nobody knew what she was doing, either. They came closer the homestead and collected two lemons because they needed those, too. They were tossed into the dress of the sister, and they were taken back to the homestead.

Santeia was in the capital L courtyard with the old man, who was her great uncle. Everything was ready for the cooking to start. At some point, chicken was smelled in the capital L courtyard. Also, the potatoes were cooked. Everybody was outside, in the jocular revels, and it was repose, too. The typical Kassitera Levanah were out, again. The night was consumed and it became of lesser happenings—people had trodded back to their bedrooms—and the plantation workers, Tina and her sister, and their parents, among a number of other plantation workers, went to slumber in their houses, and said goodbye, slow, and trickling out into the roads.

Panagiotis found himself in bed. It was late, and everybody had gone away; if it were the same colloquy as it was earlier, nobody could get away with folly. The colloquy had broken down into smaller colloquies; people were dipping in and out of rooms. Santeia came into the loft, where Panagiotis slept in the nights. She undressed and flipped the covers. She got Panagiotis naked to his butt, and then mounted him, with her feet and with her tits.

Santeia did open wide the blinds. The cotton sheet had been pulled over Santeia, again. This time, it had been dyed by aniline; the window tinted the astral light, the Levanah spilling on her face. The Helios bowed around the Atlantic and Americas.

1453

The dinner preparations were already in motion. Pantagathus had just gone inside for the bread Tavis, the heretic, had mentioned in the figs. He and the girl he had met, last night in the festivities, followed Tavis, the heretic, into the kitchen. Yves Albatrois, maker of guitars, was sitting at the kitchen table and eating bread.

"Have a seat, Pantagathus."

"Thanks." Pantagathus sat down. "This is Rhode." He gesticulated to the girl behind him.

"We know each other," said Yves Albatrois, maker of guitars.

"Good," said Pantagathus.

"We should all be in such good company," said Yves Albatrois, maker of guitars. "I have lost track of Patri."

"She is around the homestead," said Pantagathus. "She is a good girl."

"It helps me sleep at night."

"How did you sleep?"

"I didn't sleep last night."

"We need preparations for the dinner, the big dinner."

"The corn fields need to be visited."

"Send Rhode," said Pantagathus.

Rhode slapped his shoulder. "We will go together after this," said Rhode.

"Very good," said Yves Albatrois, maker of guitars. "Take that basket with you." He pointed to the basket in the corner of the kitchen. They ate breakfast, and then Pantagathus and Rhode went to the corn fields.

"I counted fifty people last night," said Pantagathus. "There are about twenty now."

"They are a wayward lot."

"Twenty savage people," said Pantagathus.

"People will return," said Rhode.

"I am glad I brought this wine." Pantagathus held up his wine skin. They walked past a tree stump and a pair of leather gloves. There had been three bags of wine Pantagathus was addressing all night. This was the only one remaining. There had been many wine skins. Pantagathus and Rhode walked past the people in the fig fields.

In small rooms, throughout the Byzantine capital, the outcome of all epochs had been destroyed. The assumption of vapor, and then the subsequent manifestations of collagen were in small rooms, throughout Constantinople, not during the festivities, but three months prior; and they were of a certain body of altered composite. There was an equated parallel. Those who were of altered composite were literal embodiments of writings and people and of the formulaic ideas, which were of every week on Σάββατο—the chopped architecture had been chopped by hands and those hands touched the iconoclast people, and left the iconoclast people defiled—with chips of stone and silver where the face would be and chips of stone and silver where the package would be, and there was the lustre sliding off of the busts of girls and expressionless composure, while the people to the east attacked and did snag the punctual ones, the people, whom they did forn. There was no answer, upon summons, and the acquaintances walked in and met the once assuaged by loofa bodies. The acquaintances saw the answer for which they had been looking—Where is this girl?—and found, instead of the high, respectable, and reverent girl of the body of gold, a pit, which was the remnants of a person, who was of gold and body, and who was of spectacle for Yo'he'vah'he— all Φιλλαλιλία and all hours.

Pantagathus glanced at Rhode, and he did perceive the coarse hair of her person as the topography of mind. He saw in Rhode a girl, who was young, and who was in want of peculiar occurrences and discourse, all of which seemed the be the case over the past three months, and which she seemed to have found. The substantial head was the bramble of the homestead, through which they walked, towards the corn field. There were small differences in the two, Rhode looking through a thin sheen and into the world, and Pantagathus in the troposphere and of ambivalence; the topography was beginning to take differences. It had begun to make discrepancies, in between items and people and bodies, gold and otherwise, and more so than it had in the former millennium, because chaos has descended, and all were beginning to see the alterations. Rhode glanced back at Pantagathus, who saw her eye through a membranous palate of water, which was of the upwards and downwards directions—her eye had just breached it—and he saw a glimpse of her.

They had reached the corn field, and Pantagathus began depositing into the basket ear of corn after ear of corn. He would not have minded bringing an extra bag to collect ears of corn for their home southwards. The basket was filled with ears of corn, and Pantagathus buried his heel in the red earth.

1923

Panagiotis and Santeia lay like two brush strokes. The Levanah were moderate in their luminescence. Santeia lay asleep, while Panagiotis mused of Tassi and the burros and wagon. The temperature was leveling at 11 degrees Centigrade. It was October, and it had been agreeable. The window blinds were still open. The window remained closed. Panagtios got out of bed and put on his khakis.

Panagiotis went outside and Harito was sitting on the patio, in the capital L courtyard. Harito was drinking a bottle of whiskey. He was drinking, and he was noticeable in his drunkenness, when Panagiotis approached.

Harito said, "How goes your evening?"

Panagiotis said, "It is well, and you have been enjoying yourself, with your drink?"

"Yes, I am. Have a drink."

Panagiotis said, "Sure," and he took a drink from the bottle of whiskey. There was dry meat on the table. Panagiotis had a bite of dry meat. "The evening has turned out well, the whiskey or no."

Stefangianopoulou came outside, from the homestead.

Panagiotis said, "—and Stefangianopoulou joins."

Stefangianopoulou said, "Good evening." He sat down on one of the last two chairs in the courtyard, and said, "I have come to drink the last of the bottle of whiskey."

"Join us," said Harito.

"—and have a smoke." Stefangianopoulou pulled out tobacco and paper. It was grass paper. Also, he pulled out matches, and, when he was done rolling his cigaro, he lit it up. They were close to have finished the whiskey and Stefangianopoulou got up and went to the stone fence. He looked out onto the street of Kassitera, which undulated, and which changed. He stood there for five minutes. He came back and his smoke was finished. He grabbed the dry meat and took a drink from the bottle. All of them took from the dry meat and took a few drinks.

Panagiotis got up and went back inside to the bedroom. Santeia was still lying in the bed. She was not asleep. Panagiotis lay down, and Santeia started talking. Panagiotis did not remember anything of it. He did not remember what she said.

In the morning, Panagiotis fed the heads of sheep. He went to the corral, and the heads of sheep were well, and Zito and Zuny were in the shed, with their pups. They were clean and very small. On the way out of the barn, Panagiotis put more feed. Panagiotis was walking back to the homestead; he walked past the lemons and the distillery.

It was late in the morning; the Helios was at near apex. A rider was riding up the road. Panagiotis regarded them and went to sit down, in a chair. They grew nearer, and Panagiotis looked and noticed there were two riders. Both were on one specimen Equus caballus; the specimen Equus caballus was nearer, and the rider stopped in the front of the capital L courtyard, on the opposite side of the stone fence, and it was his mother, whom he was without, and whom he was to attempt to contact, with the usage of the stamps of Harito. The rider, who was a male, got off the specimen Equus caballus and helped the mother of Panagiotis off the specimen Equus caballus. She was quiet and walked towards the gates.

Panagiotis said, "Mama."

"I have come here to find you and I've found you."

"How did you know to come to Kassitera?"

The mother of Panagiotis said, "I was traveling in the backwards direction to find you. We were in the front of the procession. We sent Giorgos to go towards the front to insure it was so. He went and found the front close by. We decided then which way to head, in search of you."

Panagiotis said, "Oh?"

"We came to a wagon, and outside of the wagon was flitting the linens, our linens, and I went to the back of the wagon and found a boy there."

"Tassi."

"Yes, Tassi; and he told me you had given him the wagon and the burros, because you and three others had headed off to Kassitera." She came into the capital L courtyard. "Brazen cries scored the air our last night in Constantinople, and your father, a warrior, was killed." The mother of Panagiotis wore the dark shawl. "We delivered him into his crypt, and there his mother stayed for a time alone."

Panagiotis ran his fingers through his coarse hair. He had ridden through the arches, which had been before him, and which did lead into a land between two hands, Athanatos the immortal, and the jeopardizor, who had taken his blood and spilt it on the grounds. He was young and still did not understand the conflicts of that great city, but he would, because he had left and had been brought into the mouth of a lion, to be hardened by its bite and to wizen, and it was to deliver Panagiotis to the peculiar heavens. Panagiotis, swift, had gone through the arches. The burros did kick behind them sand, and they covered up the preceding tracks of the undeniable crowd, which had taken silence, and which was protecting a secret, Panagiotis meandering through the people, with pansophism. He was still too young to speak of it, in earnest. All were a part of the processions. The cypresses swayed in the wind and there was a fragrance of chamomile, with milk and with feint.

The mother of Panagiotis said, "He had been knifed in the back and a club was brought to his head." Panagiotis clenched his chin. "Perhaps you are too wise," his mother said. "It is the work of the Ecumenical Patriarchate."

The conceptions of the three months following the exit of the gate were the matter, as he went towards the north and west, towards the mountain and towards Kassitera. Kassitera had not been a possibility, not at that point; but, the exchanges and journey through Eptadendros and Kassitera were an inevitability, and Panagiotis did not know that at the time, nor would he have liked it at the time—the beacons were growing outwards and making contact with that which was the most opportune for Panagiotis, in the travels north and west, away from Constantinople and towards Eptadendros and the mountain—and the tetrapolar spores took him to a multitude of exchanges with Santeia. It had taken him to Kassitera and to the inevitable reunion, which was then occurring outside of the homestead of the old man, great uncle of Santeia, with the mother of Panagiotis and when Panagiotis was told of his father and of the expository, with hybridity. It had taken him to Kassitera, en route towards that of which the beacons had been a most contiguous presence, imperceptible and of affectation, making contact and hitting the light, over and over again. It had been repetitious and had tagged oscillated time. It was a guarantee for the hand and man, who was Panagiotis.

The mother of Panagiotis removed her sandals, and she went back out through the gates and into the street, where the mount resided. She began untying ropes. There were a few items she had brought with her from Constantinople and from the procession. The escort, Giorgos, took the bag from her hands. The escort, Giorgos, went into the capital L courtyard. He sat and rested his bony person. Panagiotis went inside, and he got a bottle of water from the kitchen and the dry meat and went back outside to the courtyard. The mother of Panagiotis and the escort, Giorgos, ate the dry meat and drank the water, and then the invention had, by Panagiotis, been mentioned, following which he took his mother to the laboratory, where she belonged.

2017

Pete Tsiminis was in the thicket of Betulaceæ, where the ravine was visible. The phonics and the exposure were omnipresent. Pete Tsiminis drank a bit of the tea and then made pee. The thicket was dense. Behind him, the Betulaceæ was sparse. Walking straight from the Tsiminis household, straight forwards for thirty minutes, one got to the thicket, which was inclined on the left-hand side, and which had an impression on the right-hand side. The specimens Betulaceæ were navigable, and it was a compact thicket, and the incline and impression were the differentiation between the thicket and the start of aggressive topography, further outwards. Turn right one hundred and twenty degrees and you saw the ravine. Pete Tsiminis was beginning to sweat in his boots and scarf and long johns.

The ravine ran into the bay, that is Red Bay, with the whales and with the iron ore deposits. Pete Tsiminis looked out into the ravine and drank some more tea. A broken specimen Betulaceæ was lain on the ground. It was propped up on its stump, and it was supported at the other end by foliage, which made it a level bench. Pete Tsiminis sat down and opened his lunch of a grilled cheese sandwich. There was ketchup, and his mother taught him that. The hike had been thirty minutes—that was only one way—and it was to be another thirty minutes, back to the house, where his parents may well be searching for him and concerned, his father smoking and his mother in the kitchen, or dusting, or cleaning dishes. Upstairs, rooms were untouched. The poster from the Museum of Modern Art, the metallic apple, the brass spoon, and the reconstrued skeleton; his hamper and sink and bureau; the window, which allowed a look downwards, towards the sack of firewood, covered in ghost white, and out through into the Betulaceæ, which went out fifteen kilometers, until they became maples, and which numbered five hundred thousand in this wood, alone, in Newfoundland and Labrador; the shoes and the can full of markers—all were maintained, and they were unmalleable. One thousand and one paces away, a pin dot was peering over into the ravine. He was swollen and vermillion. He looked down and into the ravine, and he would have liked to have seen a trout or a pelican. It was the electric sounds of the ravine, which arose upwards, and also the humidity.

The essence was finding him. It was the essence of the ravine. It was the essence of the Betulaceæ. It found him today, as it had every day, from its elevated vantage. There had been a collision, and it was noticeable in the smallest of ways, the rising scent of the snow; the electrical phonics of the ravine; the acoustics of those Betulaceæ, which were quite at hand; and also the biologies of Animalia, hither and yon, and the biology of Pete Tsiminis—all of which celestial masses bounded through time, unashamed and restless. The immediacy of it all scored the air. Pete Tsiminis had the ages and light as his ally, as he delivered an embrace to the flipped camaraderie, which had, having exchanged places with the corners of his being, guided Pete Tsiminis through the numerous δεισιδαιμονία of nascence and laxness and blithe nightingales, which he had gone too long without, which had been given to him in pieces, and which he had lain together and passed whole back to it, as it found him that afternoon, as it always had since the two collided, in his spectral dreams.

He took off his glove and reached down to pick up a rock. He weighed the rock in his hand and tossed it up and down in his hand, four or five inches, each time, and by four times; and then he shucked the rock outwards into the ravine. He slung it outwards and did not follow its trajectory downwards, with his eyes. He looked at it only as long as he was able to look at it, outwards and until the rock, with eventuality, bowed down and away, out of the field of vision. Pete Tsiminis was quite ready to start back home. The thirty-minute walk was to arrive him, in proper. Pete Tsiminis had picked up his nylon glove and had put it back on his hand. He looked out at the ravine and the plutonical slab, both of which were visible through the interstice of the specimens Betulaceæ. The Betulaceæ, inklings from the abberant and from the insentient, did assume their insitu, a motionless return back to their excrescence. They were not to be travestized, nor were they to be altered. The Betulaceæ had been acidified. It was high noon. The flurries had begun to fall.

About the Author

Anders M. Svenning was born in New York. His work has appeared in numerous magazines. He authored several books. *50 States Poetry* (Pansophic Press), *Verdant Grounds, Subtle Boundaries* (Adelaide Books) are two books, which have been released, and he has forthcoming pieces, too, *We Are Inmate #881129* (Wild Dreams Publishing), *The Phrenologist* (HellBound Books), *Occipital Circus & Other Stories Regarding Phrenology* (HellBound Books), *Life After Schizophrenia* (Scarlet Leaf Publishing).

www.ingramcontent.com/pod-product-compliance
Lightning Source LLC
Chambersburg PA
CBHW021010120726
47905CB00009B/2944